# Noble Creek

## Tom LaPorte

Heliopolis Publishers
Las Cruces, NM

Noble Creek

All rights reserved.  © 2007 by Tom LaPorte

No part of this story may be reproduced, stored in a
retrieval system or transmitted in any form or by
any means without the prior written permission of
Tom LaPorte.

All characters appearing in this work are completely
fictitious.  Any resemblance to real persons, living
or dead, is purely coincidental.

ISBN:  978-0-6151-6910-1

Published by **Heliopolis Publishers**
Las Cruces, NM

Printed in the United States of America

Tom LaPorte

I0671804

To John, Daryl, John, Bruce and Natalie.
Thanks for the inspiration.

Greetings!  As a teacher, I often tell my students,
"You are never finished when writing."  I am
thankful to the many people who gave of
themselves to read various drafts of this book, made
corrections and offered editorial feedback in my
long journey with this project.  I'm particular
thankful to Shannan who remains ever optimistic
and supportive.

## Introduction

If only I'd taken out the trash. If anybody had taken out the trash at least every once and a while. No, it's nobody else's fault. It's all me. I'm to blame. Pastor Frank was right. I was born in sin and there wasn't any good in me. I knew it was wrong. I knew all my headaches, stomachaches, nightmares and embarrassment stemmed from the house. I knew it caused my brother's torment. Yet, I did nothing. None of us did a thing.

We let the garbage pile up and go from bad to unbelievable. We managed to conceal our dirty secret for as long as I could remember. Now the horrible truth has been revealed and it's all my doing. I should have listened to my mama and did what she told me to do during the snowstorm. I did everything wrong. All I had to do was let the stupid pipes drip. Then I could have done whatever I wanted. Just this once, I should have done what she said. But, like an idiot, I had to do it my way.

My eyes welled. I felt like crying. I didn't. I couldn't. I gazed out of the newly replaced window in the Ford Granada. We rode in tandem, sandwiched between two police cars. I felt like a criminal of major proportions. The officers said the caravan was for my own protection, but I knew they expected me to make another run for it. The same officer of the court sat next to me in the back seat. She talked a lot. I ignored her and stared out the window.

"Would you like to stop for something to eat? It's going to be a while before we can get you settled in foster care," she said. I didn't like the idea of foster care and gave thought to an escape plan.

I looked up as the Granada drew close to a bridge crossing a creek. I knew that bridge. Oh, how I knew it and the wonderful body of water it crossed. It was Carp Bridge. Like so many times before when I found myself in the midst of self loathing and cursing the world around me, this majestic place came to me. I felt the edges of my mouth forming a smile. Oh its beauty, its intrigue! The creek was the one thing I couldn't mess up. Not even acts of God could destroy this hallowed place. It's where I escaped my world and appreciated the goodness in the world around me. The creek was the place where I came to appreciate nature and the seasons.

"So the idea of food appeals to you?" she asked, mistaking my facial expression.

"No. I'm not hungry right now." I replied.

"Why the smile?" she asked.

"I'll tell you if you really want to know." She twisted in the seat and looked at me attentively, and so I began.

"We just crossed Carp Bridge. I lived a great deal of my life under that very bridge." The woman got all pie eyed. I recognized her horror and let the woman know it wasn't as she thought. I hadn't actually lived there, though it might well have been better if I had. Man, how I loved that place. I thought about the seasons. I thought about change. I thought about how at the creek I had changed with the seasons.

# Spring
## Chapter 1

I remember as a boy I had to stay home while my brother, Duke, went walking around after school or during the summer. He called it cruising. Everyday I begged him to take me. Not only did my mom forbid it, but my brother thought it uncool to have a bratty little kid trailing behind him. So, he readily shot down my daily pleas. Once, though, out of the blue, he announced it was time for me to learn my way around the neighborhood. That day he and a couple of his friends went to the creek to smoke dope. They sat under the bridge and got high. Duke forced, and I do mean forced, me to keep a distance in order to avoid smoke contact.

They finished smoking. Now the fun came as all of us waded down the creek. As unexpectedly as his invitation to cruise with him, my brother hurled me into a deep part of the creek.

"Help me! I can't swim!" I cried.

"Swim or drown, sissy. Only sissies don't know how to swim," he said.

Laughing, he told me to find my way home and then he took off with his buddies. I managed an ugly version of the dog paddle and pulled myself ashore using a root. After crying and being lost for a bit, I discovered I loved the place. So I lingered.

I obsessed about going back. Mama wouldn't let me walk as far as the creek by myself. So, I begged Duke to take me with him every day. Each and every time he did something mean to me. Once he put me on a tire swing and pushed me so hard I though the rope would loop around the branch on which it hung. I was too afraid to jump back on the bank. I gripped the rope with all I had. Eventually, the momentum of the swing stopped and I had no choice but to let go and fall into the creek. The water ran deep there, but I had learned some semblance of swimming from all the other times my brother flung me in the creek.

As far back as I could recall I had been going with him to the creek, even though I knew good and well Duke and his buddies were going to terrorize me in some way. No matter what, I kept coming back for more. I loved the creek and I wanted to be with my brother more than anything. If abuse was the only attention I got from him, I took it, gladly.

## Chapter 2

As I grew older mama would let me walk to the creek with a friend. She didn't want me down there alone. She kept telling me about how some weird old dude had cut up two boys by the railroad track before I was even born. All the parents in my neighborhood would revisit the tale when kids were out after dark or out alone.

That worked out fine, so in time I took all of my friends to the creek. Everybody thought it rocked. There's this one place where you can look down from the bridge over the creek. Two large carp remained visible nearly all the time. Regardless of what bait we tried, the carp never bit our lines. The fish sat there, uninterested, and seemed to mock our attempts to catch them. Hence, we called it Carp Bridge.

Over the years we wore a trail alongside of the bridge as our main passage to the creek. Under the bridge we took off our shoes and socks before wading or swimming in the creek. We took shelter from the rain under the bridge and enjoyed the shade in the hot southern summers. In the support beams of the bridge we hid our fishing poles.

I remember this one time at Carp Bridge when I got really pissed off and yelled at my buddies.

"It had to be one of you," I shouted at my friends. "Y'all know we ain't supposed to steal from each other. You have to take care of your own. That's what my brother says."

"Your brother's a psycho," Bubba proclaimed.

"Yeah, but he'd whip your ass just for saying so," I said, and jumped down from the middle support under the bridge. Being tender footed stunk. Even the smooth water-polished rocks sent spikes of pain into the bottom of my feet. I cursed after the splash landing.

"Calm down, Fat Boy. Why would we steal our own fishing rods?" Silo asked harshly.

Most everybody in my neighborhood had a nickname. The names originated from something at school or what your mother called you at home. To my dismay, I was Fat Boy, not a very creative thing to call an overweight kid. Most folks referred to my brother as Duke. Everybody assumed he came by the moniker because like the legendary John Wayne, my brother had been a hellion from the womb. Unfortunately, I knew the ugly truth. The first song my brother liked was the oldie, *Duke of Earl*. He loved the tune and would sing the chorus incessantly. Mama said it was the only endearing thing he ever did. So she called him Duke and it stuck.

My buddies were Silo, short for Silas, Bubba and MD. Bubbas filled our neighborhood. We had tons of them. In my grade level alone we had Bubba Wiggins, Bubba Jones, Bubba Grier and our Bubba. My brother had two or three Bubbas within his circle of friends as well. One of the better nicknames was Caddie. My classmate, David SaVille, came about the name as it sounded like Seville, as in the Cadillac. My best friend went by MD. That stood for Melvin Defore, although he preferred to think of himself as Mad Dog. My other friend Paul stood out as the odd ball. He simply went by Paul. He was quite the character nonetheless.

Still fuming, I marched quietly out of the creek as the severity of Silo's question settled on me. I kicked my bare foot in the sand. I looked around the banks of the creek and announced, "This has been the worst spring break ever."

"Oh stop your cryin' and let's do something," Bubba said.

"We can hunt for golf balls to sell to the rich old men," Silo suggested. None of us responded. We stood there looking goofy on the sandy beach-like area of the creek at the base of Carp Bridge.

"Let's head up the creek to the drop off and go swimming," MD offered another option.

"Aw, hell no! It's too cold. I can wade in it, but my nads aren't going in this ice water," I said. I lied in part. I did hate the cold but the real problem stemmed from the fact that I never became a fluid swimmer and the guys poked fun at me.

So, we sloshed through the chilly water trying to find golf balls. We spent much more time turning over rocks looking for salamanders and crawdads than golf balls. After a spell we toted our haul of golf balls on to the green. The market favored us that day. We took about a quarter per ball and we sold most of our inventory. Only a half dozen or so remained. We paced around until we found a couple of white haired golfers who showed an interest in the last of our bargain balls.

"I'll give you a nickel for two balls," one of the old guys said. "What do you say, kid?"

"I say kiss my boney ass," Bubba said, poking out his thin bird cage chest.

"Why, you little punk," the older man said, brandishing his golf club.

"You ain't gonna do shit with that club. I'll bust your old ass if you even think about swinging that thing at me," Bubba threatened.

The man surged forward. Bubba smacked the guy and we chucked the golf balls at both of the men. Bubba gave the other guy a kick and then we all ran like rabbits. The geezers offered no challenge and we counted the getaway as another successful escape to our perfect record. Puffed up and feeling cocky, we went to the local convenience store and spent all of our golf ball salvage earnings. We bought Cokes, junk food and played video games into the evening.

Time to head home always came, though; I always tried to wish it away. Like every other night I stayed out as late as I dared. Finally, I sucked it up and went to the house. Standing outside the door I took note of the stillness of the night. It seemed weird. I didn't hear the crickets and an eerie wind blew amidst the calm. I took one more glance at the vastness of the sky and strolled through the crap that welcomed me home every night. The long day of goofing around wasn't enough to wear me out. I knew sleep wouldn't come immediately.

## Chapter 3

I kept trying to jump off the train. My heart pounded in my chest. My throat constricted. All of my body parts did the wrong thing and none of them did what I wanted. I couldn't move. I saw MD standing in the middle of the railroad tracks. He stood still and yet he rapidly moved further and further away. My hands tingled with numbness and I dropped the bucket of road flares and other stuff we had stolen from the train, but still the ability or the courage to jump didn't come. The train roared on and MD grew tiny in the distance. Out of the tree line, a hooded man ran and snatched MD by the waist and carried him into the woods. I willed my body to simply fall forward without the benefit of a lunge or thrust.

I gasped as I awakened. My mom called out to me and our tiny house shook as if being uprooted by the very hand of God. Lightening flickered rapidly and lit up the sky. It didn't seem real. I thought my eyes were adjusting. I heard a sound reminiscent of the roaring of a train. Something terrible was coming directly for us. In the darkness and my disorientation I made out my mother saying, "It's coming right over the house. We don't have time to go to the basement." She didn't have to say any more. In an instant I knew either a tornado was coming or the rapture was here. I hoped upon hope for the twister. I wasn't ready for Jesus.

I rolled off my bed and went to crawl underneath it. Like in my dream, I froze. Once more the power to command my muscles to move eluded me. I found myself face to face with the biggest spider I had ever seen. The eight legged vermin had stripes or lines on its back and a thick sticky web that I felt cling to my skin. I swatted at the spider and managed only to invite it directly onto my face. In that moment, the spider presented a far greater horror to me than the tornado. To me the devastating funnel of wind with all its power remained only an abstract idea. The spider brought an immediate and corporal terror. In my mind the spider had attacked and was ready to strike. I regained the ability to move and flipped around on the floor in a pile of clothes, food wrappers, plastic containers and crumpled papers. All the while I slapped at my face with all the vigor in my body.

Within minutes I had moved from a nightmare into the eye of a storm and finally to torment from a creature I dreaded. The spider didn't bite me. No, it did something far worse than that. It escaped. I never found the spider, dead or alive. It wasn't due to a lack of effort. I hunted it wildly. I sifted through the piles of junk around and under my bed. My mom was screaming for me to get down. I couldn't get under the bed or on the floor until I found the object of my trepidation. I peeled the web from my hair and I knew the spider had been real. My fear was real and it worsened as I couldn't find the spider.

I didn't sleep in that bed or in that room ever again. I moved into our basement the very next day. In fact, sleep grew very problematic for me. The memory of that night, of that spider lingers. I hate spiders. I kill them. I can't even handle imagining the threat they pose. If I see one, I must see it die so that I will know it can't get me.

## Chapter 4

The wake of the storm was no better than my lost battle with the oversized spider. The tornado devastated the spindly Georgia pines in our neighborhood. Leaves, limbs and mature trees lay strewn all over the place. Morning illuminated the multiple trees that lay crisscrossed in our yard. We went outside and discovered that one had fallen directly on the right side of our front porch. I stood dressed and ready for school, staring in disbelief at the wreckage. I figured we could saw the tree, but I really wanted to know where that spider had crept to in the night.

"We're late. I'll tend to this later," my mama said, referring to the fallen tree. Whenever mama had a car, we ran late. If she had to ride the bus you could set your watch on her. I didn't think I'd be marked tardy this morning with the storm and all. We drove away from the house and into the rain and wind, leaving the tree still pressed against the house. As we rode, life moved in slow motion. I pressed my face to the car window and looked on in shock at Interstate guard rails in the courtyard of a church, and roof shingles lining the streets and gutters. Street signs lay twisted and mangled. I tried to decide if it was actually a bumper from a car that I saw wrapped high on a power pole.

"Sweet Jesus!" my mom cried out. I whipped my head around. Life went from slow motion to stopping altogether. A gaping hole decorated my elementary school. Police and other emergency personnel directed traffic. The damage was so bad that all the students from my school met in a church that day and we were rerouted to another school for the rest of the school year.

I had become intimately aware of the violence and destruction of the tornado. It tore up buildings and other things in my neighborhood. The powerful winds ripped a corner off the roof of our school. Even with a tree smashed against my house I hadn't thought of a natural event like a tornado wreaking havoc on nature itself. It did. Acts of God bringing injury on God's own creation simply baffle me.

Branches, plants and wind driven debris mucked up the banks and clogged the creek in several places. Trees fell across the rolling water and created bridges. Later I came to appreciate the storm bridges, as we called them, as in many places the creek had a width similar to a river. Tree trunk cross-overs grew in appeal, especially in the colder months.

I didn't understand the concept of hurting your own. As far back as I remember, Duke always taught me to take care of your own. He said nobody cared about helping poor people, so we had to help ourselves. I reckoned this same theory should hold for animals and nature as well as people.

A yellow film coated the waters as the rains had washed pine pollen into the creek and all about. The old tire swing Duke and his friends strung up had fallen. It bobbed like a float on a fishing line as the tree it was tied to lay split in half in the water. It was some time before my pals and I hung up a new one. We put our swing over shallow water and close to the bank. Duke said we were sissies. I didn't care.

Like the symbolic phoenix of Atlanta, something good rose from the tornado's wreckage. While taking in the damage of the storm and pondering the mysteries of life, I discovered an old utility building on the banks of the creek. Like the environment, the creek and the storm, the find of the abandoned structure changed my life forever.

Changing schools pretty much stunk. Mostly rich kids attended the substitute school. They didn't like us being there any more than we wanted to be there. The only good part of the relocation came from the walk home. The path from the new school took us past a different portion of the creek, one we hadn't explored previously. That worked out well. The banks were higher there. The water was deeper as well, and this made for our version of a high dive and many a cannon ball and belly flop. We also developed a passive aggressive stand off with the plaid shorts boys on the new route. These were kids who looked to be about our age and played golf wearing ridiculous outfits. We thought the ugly shoes and goofy pants were a riot.

Bubba and Silo made out like they wanted to beat up the plaid shorts boys every time we saw them playing in their fancy plaid shorts and funny shoes. Like us, the plaid shorts boys kept words and fists to themselves. We all shot glances and disapproving looks like weapons of war. I knew the slightest little mumble would have been the trigger to pounce on each other. My friends and I fought regularly. We fought rich kids, jocks and other low rent punks like ourselves who went to rival schools, but we never hooked it up with the plaid shorts boys. I'm not sure why we avoided a ruckus with them.

## Chapter 5

"The good suffer with the wicked!" Pastor
Frank extolled as if he had written the Bible verses
himself. He pounded his heavy fist on an old
wooden pulpit. "I tell you, the son toils for the
father's sins." The preacher dabbed a stained
kerchief on his forehead and both corners of his
lips. That meant he was about to bring it home. He
did the same thing every Sunday without fail.

"The good Lord used that terribly swirling
tornado as His agent. The good Lord passed over
His beloved and punished those who sin and the
ones with sin in their hearts. And let me tell you,
sinner, the Lord's arm is outstretched, ready to
strike again. Brethren, don't let it be. Do not let it
be. Repent. Repent now. Repent!"

Clearly, Pastor Frank had not visited the
creek. The hand of the Lord had worked damage
there just the same as everywhere else. Sure, my
mama, brother and I were sinners and deserved to
be hit by the storm. Our sin brought that tree down
on our rickety house. But the creek was a sinless
work of beauty from God's own hand, the same
hand that crushed much of nature with the holy
agent of the whirlwind.

Pastor Frank took off his watch and
carefully placed it on the pulpit next to his tattered
Bible. The small brick church sweltered. I swear I
saw heat radiating in the room. The ladies fanned
themselves with the service bulletins. One of the
deacons opened a window close to his pew.

"Brethren, I know the hour is late. But
friends, you know time is of the flesh. We must
listen to the signs the good Lord has put to us. Now
I need every head bowed and every eye closed. I

beg of you.  As Sister Jean plays, won't you come forward?  Won't you come down and be washed in the blood of the lamb?  Listen, sinner, the next storm may take your life." Pastor Frank paused and dabbed at his mouth again.  "If it does, where will you go?  Will you be in the bosom of the Lord or will you burn in a lake of fire for all eternity?  The time is now.  Repent!"

I didn't know for sure where I'd go if I died. I didn't know anything of my father's sin like Brother Frank had preached about.  But I knew for sure it was my sin, the sin of my family and our house that brought on the storm.  There was no doubt in my mind.  I didn't want anyone to get hurt. I didn't want the creek to be damaged anymore.  I got up and threw myself on the mercy of the altar. Hands and tongues of the faithful went to work. They said I had been remade into a new creature in Christ.  They said I was saved.  I prayed in hopes of saving the creek.

## Chapter 6

Out of nowhere and right in the middle of a heated rock skipping contest, Christy Hillshire appeared at the creek. Not only was she a girl, she was a nasty girl. Her clothes stunk of moth balls and her stringy hair looked greasy and clung to her head. Christy was older and stood taller than any of us. Her gangly stature, yellow teeth and chronic bad breath made her a walking stigma.

Silo, MD, Bubba and I ran her off. We threw rocks at her on sight. Mr. Accuracy himself, Silo, hit her in the leg. Christy splashed through the water and disappeared into the brush. My mind flashed to the hooded man by the railroad from my dreams, the one who in real life had captured children and cut them up. I let it go quickly, though, as we were nowhere near the railroad track and the only victims had been boys, not girls.

We went back to our game, zipping smooth rocks across the water and laughing at weird nasty Christy.

"I bet that was the first bath she's had all year," Bubba said.

Images of Christy had nearly faded when she replaced them by bounding out of the woods, stark naked. Albeit she was tall and awkward, Christy undeniably had nice, round breasts. Her freckled skin stretched tight on her nubile body. A dark tuft of pubic hair stood out like a target on her pale figure.

"Come on. You can do what ever you want with me. I can take all of y'all," she announced.

Suddenly, she didn't seem so repulsive to any of us. We took turns going around the bend to be with her. I drew the short straw and ended up last. Surprisingly, it didn't take long to get a turn. I had already gone to work on myself trying to find a cool way to back out. Being last sucked. Being afraid would be worse. I felt like I was on stage for Christy and for my friends, and I had a hint of stage fright.

I crept around the bend and Christy waved to me. She sat as naked as you please in the sand. She called to me, "Come on, Fat Boy, I won't bite. I promise."

Without any other words I pulled down my shorts and lay down with her. After a couple of minutes I moved on top of her. I felt sure that this was not how it was supposed to be for my first time having sex. I forged on and entered her. We bumped and pushed out of sync for all of five minutes.

"Why are you letting us do this to you?" I couldn't help but to ask while still inside of her.

"My brother says since I have carpet and knobs I should be doing it," Christy said frankly.

"Your brother sees you naked?" I asked, mortified.

"Yeah. All the time. We don't do it. I mean we don't go all the way. He watches me get dressed and stuff. Sometimes he pinches my boobies and butt. That's all."

I stopped moving. Pressing my hands in the sand I pushed back and looked at her face for the first time since I had come around the bend.

"Do your folks know about that? You know, about your brother grabbing at you?" I asked.

"I don't know. I never said anything. I guess they know. We all go around without clothes sometimes. It's no big deal. We're family, so it's okay. Danny says everybody does it. So, I figured if I did it with y'all, maybe you guys would pay me attention like he does."

I felt nauseated. I held myself in contempt and grew disgusted with my friends and Christy's perverted family. Her twisted brother, Danny, was older than me and younger than Duke so I didn't really know too much about him. What I did know was that in my mind he had a beating coming and I cherished the notion of giving it to him.

I had long since lost momentum. I felt myself slide out and embarrassment settle in on me. I had no idea about protocol in this sort of a situation. I felt uneasy. A slight breeze eased across my exposed bottom. Our sweat-lined bodies made an awful suction sound as I finally heaved my torso off of her. I rolled over and pulled up my shorts. I didn't know what to do with her or how to go back to my friends. I wondered if I should go back with them after what had happened, although I certainly didn't know what to say to her if I stayed.

"I'm sorry, Christy," I said for lack of anything better.

"For what? I'm happy. You were my first. Bubba didn't do nothin'. He just dry humped me. Your little gay friend Silo couldn't get it up. And that little freak MD... Well, he didn't do anything to me. You were my first, ever."

I held my breath and tried to breathe all at once. My eyes glazed over. Rorschach images flashed in my head. In an instant I felt victorious for losing my virginity and despicable for taking Christy's. I felt happy to have done the deed, but didn't understand why I also felt so terribly vulgar. I didn't know if I should thank her, provide an obligatory compliment or dispose of her.

"You ought to get dressed and go on home," I said and walked back toward my buddies.

"How was it, Fat Boy? Did you make that dog howl?" Silo asked.

"Aw, he didn't do anything. He probably sat over there and talked to her about the creek or his head case brother," Bubba added.

"All right, you two little homos. I know what happened when y'all were there. Don't make me broadcast it," I said. "Dig this, fellas, y'all know Duke's freakin' touched, but if any of you ever crack another joke about him again, I'll bust you up. You can believe that."

I thought order had been restored. How naïve. Silo started hurling rocks at Christy as she was leaving. Luckily, his accuracy failed him for once. I ran and slammed him to the ground.

"Damn, y'all! Give the girl a break!" I yelled.

I left and walked her home. I watched my feet in silence the entire way. When we got to her house, without preamble, I kicked the snot out of Danny. So much for chivalry. I never talked to Christy again. In fact, I actively ignored her. A year or so later, her daddy up and left the family in a bind, so her mother took the kids and went back to be with her people in Columbia, South Carolina. I didn't even say goodbye.

I never forgot her. Not because she was my first sexual encounter, but because my friends started called me NT for a while. It took some time before I learned that the initials stood for *No Taste*. I deserved it. Not for losing my virginity to an uncouth and bizarre girl, but for doing that which I detested. I had turned on her. Christy was a lot like me. We both hurt and we hurt ourselves. I didn't need to be her boyfriend, but I should have stood by her.  Doing what I did hurt my own kind and Duke always said that wasn't acceptable.

# Summer
## Chapter 7

Change. Change. Change. The previous spring of that year marked my life like a branding iron. I still can't believe how one stormy night had shifted so much of my entire life. A matter of minutes set a course that shaped my phobias, my sense of security and awareness of nature. The latter two came at the creek.

Our household dynamic changed. Near the end of the school year, my brother got sent away, again. This had happened a time or two before. Mama said he went to get professional help, whatever that meant. We all had problems; his were worse. He had no management of anger. He got very angry, very easily and that manifested itself in regular and intense bouts of violence. My mom never talked about Duke's situation, and neither did he for that matter. Rage worked itself through all of us, but it wholly owned my brother.

I guess by not acknowledging problems then in a sense they really didn't exist. That's what our family did. Come to think of it, we never mentioned anything problematic. Conflict avoidance to a fault, that described us. Off limits subjects included my brother's episodic institutionalization, my absent father and our landfill house.

Not finding the spider that night changed me forever. At first, I reacted with a desire to hunt spiders. I set out to do that very thing. Whenever I found a spider I went into a frenzy. I would find ways to disable or disorient the spiders. I smacked them with whatever I found handy and then I stomped them and twisted my foot on them, all the while screaming in a primal fury. Crushing a spider beyond recognition helped me to understand that unlike the spider of the storm, the one at hand would not be free to terrorize me ever again.

That initial spider won a battle it never really fought. I gave up my room to the victor. I couldn't sleep in that room or anywhere in the house again. All the trash in the house provided the spider with many too many hiding places and I irrationally believed it sat waiting to pounce on me. My mom didn't protest very much when I announced my plan to move down to the basement.

## Chapter 8

In our basement, three of the four ground level framed rooms had concrete floors. The entrance room was nearly filled with packed red dirt. Cinder blocks encased the entire area. Our basement did not have running water or heat. In fact, the dirt room, which provided access from the back of the house, had no door. One of the windows never had the frame and glass inserted, so all that existed was an open square cutout in the cinder blocks.

Sunlight didn't shine on any of the inner rooms. The basement was a dark, dank breeding ground for mold and mildew. Surprisingly, I never saw a spider down there, and that's all I really cared about. Our basement didn't connect via stairs to the main part of the house. I had to walk around the house to use the bathroom, but honestly I mostly just went in the backyard.

Not having easy access to a bathroom, I learned to hold it. I could go a long time and I came to almost enjoy the stomach pains and cramps. Almost. Once, while playing baseball with my friends, I had to go really badly. I passed lots of gas and all the other guys knew it was me. I stepped up to bat and I clinched with all my might. I hit the ball. The gallop to first base did me in and I lost control of my muscles. I couldn't hold it any more. I had an accident. Panic struck.

I ran home. I could only imagine what the back of my pants looked like. With each car that passed I assumed they saw my pants and knew what happened. They could see what I had done. I veered off the road and cut through the woods. I ran as fast as humanly possible to the creek. I jumped in and washed clean. I honestly felt guilty for polluting the water, but I saw no other choice.

Just being at the creek helped to settle my nerves. I stayed for a while. The walk home in wet pants held no shame. I had done that many times. Wet pants weren't worth even thinking about in comparison to the ribbing I'd get from my friends the next day. Before the pain of tomorrow arrived I still had to go home and that never sat well with me.

Among other things, the house always made me think of spiders. My spider hunt temporarily drew to a close after I encountered a spider much like the one that had invaded my bedroom, my dreams and many waking hours. This thing sat in the middle of a masterfully spun web. Many a tale abounded in my sphere of influence about this particular species. These big spiders have markings on their backs and in their webs. One local folk tale warned against having your name spoken in the presence of the spider. The story went that the Argiope spider would write any name it heard in its web and bring on curses and bad luck to that person. It never occurred to me that spiders don't speak English, let alone spell. Another neighborhood legend cautioned not to let these spiders see your teeth. I never knew exactly why, but the consequences were portrayed as dire.

When face to face with the creature I buckled, covered my mouth and ran. In time I did regain the courage to attack spiders on sight. Once I woke up and had to go to the bathroom. I padded through the basement to the open doorway of the dirt room. I intended to stand at the entranceway and urinate. My plan faltered. An intricate spider web gleamed in the doorway with drops of early morning dew. Precisely in the middle of the labyrinth a brownish round spider lay in wait for some unsuspecting prey.  This brought on the rage and the return to annihilating spiders.  It also added to my sleep depravation and arachnophobia.

I grew more and more neurotic about spiders.  Since that initial episode I don't like to have my face, back or head touched by anything or anyone.  I can feel every little piece of hair or loose string that comes in contact with my skin and it sends me back to the floor with that spider and its web on my face.  If there are spots on the wall or specks on the floor, I immediately assume they are spiders and I prepare to strike.  I became so fixated that after seeing a particular movie about spiders, I now shake all of my shoes prior to putting them on to ensure they are spider-free.

Like my obsession with arthropods, our house went from bad to worse, although none of us thought that could have been a possibility.  Wind and rain took a severe toll on the old and inferior building materials of the house.  The wood continued to rot where the tree had fallen on the house and the whole foundation shifted, causing the cinderblocks in the front left side to cave inwards.  This created a gaping hole and wind tunnel in the dirt room of the basement.

## Chapter 9

"Don't let the people outside of these walls intimidate you into sins of the flesh, my brethren. 'Intimidate,' that's when people pressure you into something using fear," Pastor Frank said. I wondered how the actions of the 'outsiders' were different from the preacher. For as many Sundays as I could remember, he had been scaring me into believing I'd spend all of eternity in a ring of fire. For years of Sundays, Pastor Frank let me know in no uncertain terms, "I was not worthy." In time I grew to believe him. I thought being saved pleased Jesus, but it didn't seem to be good enough for the preacher. As for taking part in sins of the flesh, that always felt good to me. I needed no intimidation.

We committed ourselves and the whole summer to sins of the flesh. Paul suggested we take matches and candles to the utility building near the creek. We tried to keep it dark in there as most girls found the place to be gross. Some of them were afraid of being in total darkness. The slightest light made them feel safe. That's all it took to keep them happy. That's when the real work began. We traded whispers of forever in hopes of immediate gratification.

When not chasing girls, the long summer days gave my buddies and me time to cut grass. We told our folks we were saving for school clothes since they couldn't afford name brands. Truth was we spent our little pocket change recklessly. Being broke didn't worry us like it did our parents. We bought stuff we liked and stole clothes for school.

Nature didn't corner the market on wildlife in the summer. Bees, ticks, leeches, hitchhikers, briars, Dogwood trees, and the pungent smell of

Japanese Cherry trees reminded the senses of long,
hot days.  We filled the unstructured time waging
war with bees that nested on our playground, telling
ghost stories in an abandoned cemetery and playing
ball.  We played football, baseball, basketball, but
never ever soccer.

Occasionally we spent the hot afternoons
perched in trees and hunted small animals with B-B
guns.  Once Mrs. SaVille made us clean and eat a
dove and a squirrel we shot in the woods behind her
house.  To our disgust, when we cut the bird open
we found chicken feed from Mrs. SaVille's coops
inside its stomach cavity.  We managed to choke
down a few bites.  Her lesson worked.  I never
killed an animal for sport again.  It didn't stop me
from slaying spiders.

## Chapter 10

Early in the summer, Duke came home without warning.

"All the kids say you were in Milledgeville. Were you?" I asked.

"No. That's where they keep prisoners and the nut jobs. I'm not crazy," he said. "Don't listen to those little rednecks."

"They said that mama doesn't have a husband and that's why we live in a shack."

Duke gave an agitated look and said, "You need to start running with a different crowd. Or else you need to pop a couple of them in the mouth. That'll shut 'em up."

"It's not the guys I hang out with. Silo's sister said our family is nut-so and that's why I get into trouble all the time at school and you get sent off to wherever it is you go." After I told Duke that stuff he told me to whip all their butts, except for the girl. I was supposed to beat up her brother instead. The problem was her brother was my buddy, Silo.

We quit talking and the two of us finally removed the tree from the porch. The damage to the house had increased by virtue of leaving the weight there for so long. Our haphazard removal added insult to injury. The entire front porch had begun to cave under the weight of the tree. Rain had rotted away the wood fascia boards and made an opening for the elements and insects. Duke and I covered the hole with plastic inside and out. The cheap patch job didn't hold up long at all. In no time, the outer plastic fell to the ground. Over time it got coated with dirt and debris like the strata archaeologists dig through when studying the deposits of people and places long past.

Our house didn't have central heating or air conditioning. Sometimes the gentle breezes and afternoon rains that came through the hole cooled the house during Atlanta's hot and humid summers. I learned in Sunday school that no good deed goes unpunished.

Torrential downpours marked the summer that year. Rain poured in the opening in our house. It discolored the sheetrock of the inner wall and rotted the wood of the interior floor boards and granted access to a wide variety of living creatures. Among them were rodents, mosquitoes, spiders and a cat. The latter came and went as she pleased. We fed her when possible. The feline didn't have a collar or name tag. We called her "Here, Kitty Kitty" to get her attention and she responded to it. Over the years that's what we came to call her-- Here Kitty Kitty--as a name.

Duke helped me to make the basement livable. We acquired thin sheets of foam insulation and paneling. We got them on five finger discount from construction sites. The hodgepodge materials met the immediate need. We closed off the cinderblock window and pathetically walled in one room. Duke worked so hard because he meant for the enclosed area to be his. Before we finished our work in the basement, though, they came for him. I was left without my brother, without a door in place and with heavy summer rains.

## Chapter 11

Storm water runoff flooded the creek. Yet again, nature had turned on itself. I liked it less this time than I did the first time the concept occurred to me after the tornado. The sandy banks had become packed mud. I sat on a stump of an old Magnolia tree and watched the high waters. I noticed the fish and frogs were conspicuously absent. Brown water marks scarred the formerly green plant life along the creek.

Erosion left the ground soft atop the banks of the creek. In some places it felt as though the earth might cave in at any moment, plunging down fifteen to twenty feet or more in some places. Somebody from the city or the golf club made an effort to preserve the integrity of the creek banks. They shored up edges along the water with crossties, stones and wire mesh.

I pondered the mysteries of the murky waters as they flowed so effortlessly. I recalled I had learned in church that the yearly flooding of the Nile devastated much of natural life along its banks in Egypt, yet it provided the only way for new and existing life to flourish for the remainder of the year. I hoped new and vibrant life from this flood would soon arrive.

"Whatcha doin', Fat Boy?" MD's voice startled me.

"Just thinking. I come here sometimes to hang out and think."

"Hiding is more like it," MD said.

"Whatever," I snorted. "What are you doing here alone?"

"When my old man is drinkin' or my step-mom is raising hell I come down here to get my head right."

MD and I had been friends all of our lives and never knew the other went to the creek alone. There are a lot of things I don't know, I thought. I wondered how many people were somewhere along the creek right that minute. I wondered if my brother ever came here alone.

"So you come to hide here, too?" I said, arrogantly.

"Shut up, Fat Boy!" he said. I scooted over and he plopped down on the stump with me. We were quiet for awhile. I was looking down at the water, wondering how long it would take for it to flush clear.

MD said, "You know, the creek kinda looks like a river of chocolate milk."

"Yeah, I know. There's no telling what kind of nasty stuff is flowing in front of us right this minute," I said.

MD and I got up and walked along the muddy banks. We came around a bend and a full piece of plywood drifted directly in front of us. We looked at each other. Years of being best friends allowed us to telepathically agree. Without a word we instantly went into action. We ripped off our shoes and socks and splashed toward the poor man's raft.

What a day! We rafted, swam and had a mud fight that landed us both knee deep in red Georgia clay. It took forever to free ourselves from the quasi-quicksand. Evening arrived by the time we made it back up the creek to Carp Bridge. Then we sloshed and squished our way home in the dark. MD dreaded going in his house. He knew his step-mom would kill him if he tracked in mud, silt and grossness from our Tom and Huck like adventure.

"Come on," I said. "I've got an idea. We can hose you off. Then all you have to do is hang out in your basement until you dry out a little and then you can go in the house."

That's what we did. MD took the hose to spray me down next. I refused. I didn't have to be clean to go inside. There was no reason for such in my house or the basement where I slept. We went in MD's basement, a place where we often spent time. There was only one small room, but it had electricity. The furnace that warmed the house above gave off enough heat to keep the basement warm in the cold months. MD and I talked about ways to convince the girls we liked to go to the utility building by the creek. That night we came up with a name for the building. We had covertly slipped into the dollar theater and seen the movie, *The Best Little Whore House in Texas*. Taking a cue from the film, we dubbed the utility building, "The Chicken Ranch."

"That's perfect," MD said. We can talk about it in school and stuff and no one will know it's our own little whorehouse." We laughed wildly.

We loved that our name held entertainment and sneaky appeal for our hidden love shack. The abandoned building was a far cry from romantic, but it was private. In our fantasies we could do anything the girls would let us do there without interruption. We conceived a brilliant plan on who to invite first. By then, MD's clothes were close to dry and presentable. I was sleepy, for a change. Suddenly I wanted to just lie down in MD's basement and drift off in the same way we had

eased down the waters of the creek atop the
plywood.

## Chapter 12

I was brought out of my slumber by a constant scratching of my head. "Leave me alone!" I cried out and swatted at MD's hand. Something wasn't right. Following the contact I heard a noise a few feet away. In the grogginess of sleep I couldn't tell why the feel of the contact didn't ring true. Not much later, the scratching returned. I yelled out curses and idle threats. I batted at my friend for a second time. Once again, I connected. This time the sensory information roused me to an upright position. Disorientation and confusion reigned supreme as I wiped my eyes. I was not in my MD's basement as I first thought. No, I had gone home and was asleep in my troll-like hovel.

It must have been my stupid brother pestering me. As my mind cleared I remembered Duke was in the hospital or wherever they sent him this time. I rubbed my fingertips and then I realized what was wrong. Upon contact I hadn't felt a fleshy arm, but rather something prickly and fuzzy. It couldn't have been my brother, MD or anyone.

"What the..." I howled. Visions of the big spider that had run me out of the house flashed in my head. I looked around in the dark and found two beady white eyes directed at me. We locked stares. I heard a long hiss followed by the baring of small white teeth. Mercifully, it wasn't the world's largest spider, nor was it someone irritating me. A possum had been scratching my head. Unexpectedly, I felt something moving around in the bed. There were two baby possums by my pillow. The angry mother across the room must have been trying to make a nest or bed out of my hair for her little ones.

I knew it was time to go, but the problem came in that the angry mother possum stood, poised to strike, between me and the only way out. I didn't want to kill the animal. Like me she just wanted a warm place to sleep. I threw a Coke bottle at her, to no avail. Her motherly instincts strengthened her resolve. The possum had no intention of abandoning her offspring. Duke would appreciate that level of commitment to one's own kind.

In a flash I constructed plan B. Duke may not have liked it, but I had no choice. I kicked a secondary exit through the thin paneled walls we had recently constructed. My impromptu departure held true to our family mantra--avoid conflict at all costs.

# Fall

## Chapter 13

Late to baseball practice, I hopped on my new bike, a twelve speed. I had no idea where my mom got the money for this jewel. I had been planning to steal one just like it. I peddled madly. The coach made us run laps for every minute we showed up late. Fortunately, the route to the field was mostly downhill. I rocketed through intersections and managed to get into twelfth gear. Rolling wide open, I heard a car with a road hog muffler behind me. I looked back to find a sea of traffic on my tail. I kicked harder and turned back to face the road in front of me. There I found trucks and motorcycles piled up, blocking the street. I swerved and smashed into the curb. The jolt sent me airborne. I landed and skidded along the blacktop. My body finally stopped moving right in front of a fiery red muscle car. It came to a screeching halt.

I got to my feet with no trouble at all. I stood astonished as no blood oozed from me. I should have been pulp by now. I looked up and saw angels descending and ascending. They escorted souls into heaven. Those of us left behind by the white clad cherubim roared in terror. Jesus had come and I wasn't ready.

I inventoried my bike. The front tire crumpled into unrecognizable form. The rear wheel spun and spun. A broken spoke clattered like a demonic marching drum. We, the damned, began our death walk to an eternity of Hell's wrath. Why, oh why did Pastor Frank have to be right about me?

Then reality set in from this cursed dream. However, when I opened my eyes I didn't get that feeling of instant relief knowing I had just escaped a nightmare. No, in actuality my face felt cool and wet. I had passed out. My unconscious thoughts had been both visions of the rapture picture at church and my first real life bike wreck many years ago. I cursed the subconscious and its ability to mix physical pain with the things I feared the most. Not only had the terrifying painting from church come to life in my dreams, but that first bike wreck had hurt as badly as I did presently. The reality of the bike wreck, though, had been different from the vision.

Duke had taken the training wheels off my first bike. It was very nice bicycle. I never have figured out how mama paid for it. I often considered the possibility that she was a thief just like the rest of us.

"Get on the bike, Fat Boy. You don't need training wheels," Duke said. "Those are for sissies. Are you a sissy?"

I shook my head. With that, he pushed me off. We lived at the top of a hill.

"Balance, Fat Boy, balance yourself!" Duke yelled.

I held my balance. I felt proud of not being a sissy for all of two minutes, and then I saw the bottom of the hill. Duke hadn't told me how to use the brakes. I crashed into the curb and vaulted over the handlebars. My short air flight ended with me wrapped around a telephone pole.

"Are you okay?" MD asked.

I rubbed my face and flipped out at the sight of blood smeared on my fingers. MD had dropped me to the ground after I passed out. We liked to do this thing where you squat in the catcher's position and take twenty five deep breaths. Next, you stand up and hold your breath. Meanwhile, another person grabbed up around the waist from behind and held on tight. You have to hold the air in as long as possible. I did it and went limp. MD dropped me in the church parking lot. The fall busted my chin.

When consciousness finally set in I found I had been face down in a pool of blood. I felt like I had lost a terrific amount of time. The guys laughed at me. They said it had only been twenty nine seconds. They knew because we always counted to see who stayed out the longest. I caught an earful when I got home. Mama took me to the emergency room and I got six stitches in my chin. As much as that hurt, I rejoiced that Jesus hadn't come and left me behind.

## Chapter 14

Adults clamored about the changing of the leaves every year. I didn't get why so many of them drove to all the way to the mountains to see them. A stroll along the creek provided an awesome display of auburns, greens, browns and yellows. I remember the best autumn ever. One day after school, Silo, Bubba, MD and I finally ran out of quarters and our video game fest ended. The four of us casually strolled back to our neighborhood. With no reason to hurry, we took the long way, which only added about five minutes to the route.

Silo stopped walking. Then he stepped from the sidewalk and stood in the street as a bus rolled toward him. He didn't move other than to put his hands in his jacket pocket. The bus driver blew the horn. Silo stood his ground. Seconds later he whipped a hand out and hurled something at the bus. As it crashed on the driver's side window, we realized Silo had thrown an egg. The lot of us burst out laughing. The bus's brakes locked. Still laughing, it took all of our effort to make a getaway.

We climbed a chain link fence, cut through an apartment complex and ran up a hill overlooking the roadway. With another successful escape added to our tally, we sat watching cars whiz by and tried to regain our composure. I think the surprise of Silo's miscreant attack added to the value. We never saw it coming. Silo had stolen the eggs while we were playing the video game in the store. He flung the remaining eggs he had at cars from the tactical safety of the hill.

The exhilaration of the chase and of engaging in the act of the forbidden rushed through us like pharmaceuticals. Silo would not be the only one to experience the high of deviant behavior. I wondered if Jesus ever had any fun. I knew Pastor Frank didn't. I didn't really understand how sin and redemption worked, but I knew that which was outlawed had an appeal with no equal.

We hurried to a grocery store where we purchased and stole several cartons of eggs. Eggs proved perfect; they were nature's hand grenades. We took our load of yolk-filled weaponry to the most strategic point we could think of at the time, Carp Bridge. From there we could hide in the cover of the creek side brush or under the bridge itself before blasting unsuspecting drivers with eggs. Should anyone give chase, we had the advantage of knowing the layout of the creek, the woods and the golf course where cars could not follow.

Wow, what fun we had. Before the fun ended, Silo upped the ante. A police cruiser slowed as it came to the bridge. Silo flung an egg. When common sense failed him, accuracy did not. The egg landed squarely on the cop's front windshield. The police car screeched to a halt and a spotlight went to work. Up and down the glowing beam of light swept through the shadowy night. My endorphins kicked into high gear. I spun and ran straight for the creek. I could hear the officer calling out for us to stop. *Right, like that's going to happen*, I thought. I made the mistake of looking back. The policeman had gained a lot of ground in a short time. I pumped my arms and legs with all that I had.

I knew if I crossed the creek, freedom awaited. So I swerved and headed for the babbling water. Thoughts raced in my mind as my legs did the same. My eyes settled on the narrowest part of the creek and I prayed adrenaline would give me enough superhuman strength to vault to the other side. I looked back again and my pursuer had drawn closer. I pushed with all my might.

Splash! The last step I took before leaping turned out to be the last step I took before plunging. The fall leaves had gathered along the edge of the water and I mistook them for solid ground. The loss of footing sent me hip deep into the chilly water. I never stopped moving. The police officer did. I could hear him laughing as I shimmied up the loose dirt of the sloping bank on the other side of the creek and disappeared into the cover of the woods.

In our many masterful escapes, the four of us hoodlums never had the foresight to devise a plan to meet if separated. More often than not we took separate paths to freedom. Having nothing better to do, I bit the bullet and traipsed toward my house. I felt like I'd freeze to death walking in those drenched pants. I had learned about hypothermia in school and knew for sure the chill would soon take me. I had no choice but to go into the house to warm up.

"What have you gotten yourself into?" Mama shouted.

"It's nothing." I knew better than to mention the creek in case anything was ever mentioned about the eggs or the cop. We lived in a small and meddlesome neighborhood. "We were playing down on the railroad tracks." It turned out to be a bad choice of lies on my part.

"Have you no sense a' tall? You know that's where that man snatched those two boys and cut them..." She stopped talking. She didn't want to say or to think about the fact that boys had their penises cut off by the deranged man.  The police never apprehended him.  Like the spider in the house, he remained on the loose.  I knew all the details of the case.  All the kids did.  The bad man penetrated my dreams on many occasions.

Between my self-diagnosed hypothermia, thoughts of spiders and the child killer, I felt certain I'd enter another sleepless night.  I listened to my mom drone on for several more minutes about making good choices, staying away from strangers and coming home at a decent hour.  I smiled and tried to act contrite.  I reminded her that I went to church every Sunday and she had never darkened the door.  That one worked every time.  I went to the basement and lay awake thinking about the fun of the day and tried to imagine if my life would always be one big open wound.

**Chapter 15**

Year after year I experienced fall as a season
of wonder. I have often wondered why any self-
respecting girl ever went to the Chicken Ranch with
any of our little rag tag group, but they did. Over
time we progressively moved from one girl to
another in hopes of dismantling the fortress
guarding her panties. Once we had penetrated the
walls, captured the treasure and carted off the booty,
then somehow the quest became easier. We scored
time after time with a parade of girls. Okay, so it
was only three or four. The girls smart enough to
refuse our groping and smarmy advances made up
the parade, if there in fact was a parade at all.

And then there was Rhonda. This divine
creature stood in opposition to anyone or anything I
had ever known. She had traveled, read important
books and established her own world view. Even as
a teen she was astonishingly beautiful. I met her on
a bus during a school field trip. I only ever initiated
conversation with her because my buddies shamed
me into it.

To my shock and delight, she didn't reject
my overly machismo advances. From day one, we
took off and became intense, inseparable and
passionate. We enveloped ourselves into a world
that was unconcerned with the other one that
contained six billion people and revolved around us.

Our every kiss lingered and pressed from
our lips to our inner beings. There's a John
Mellencamp song that says, "I guess every kiss
tastes sweet at 15." I know that was mostly the
case, but even now I believe that Rhonda and I
crossed a vortex of human attraction and existence.
She was close to perfect.

"I want to meet your mom and your brother. I want to know everything there is to know about you. I want to see your bedroom. Where someone sleeps tells the whole story of a person," Rhonda said.

How I remember her every word. I remember her eyes seeing me, holding me and hypnotizing me. I remember watching her facial muscles move and her jaw protrude and retract as she spoke. God, she was a vision. That's when I knew not only was she the one, she was almost perfect. No, in fact she was perfect. For every angel there is a demon. I was far from perfect. Many of my problems, like our house, were beyond my means of control to change. Nonetheless, I knew that due to my imperfections, my dearest Rhonda had to go.

Just to be with Rhonda, I had worked through my innate male fear of commitment. I dealt with my feelings of inadequacy and intimidation as compared to her worldly existence. I swallowed the queasiness that this girl invoked in every sentiment and emotion I could imagine. I handled not seeing my friends as much to be with her all the time. I accepted going to restaurants I couldn't afford and the change in movies, music and clothes; all this stuff equated to severe change to an adolescent. But Rhonda's request to see the inside of my house broke something. Something I could not fix. I couldn't even address it. It was like the words she spoke seeped into my mortal form and ripped out the sacrosanct parts of me, my darkest fears, most guarded secrets, and the ugly face I tried to keep masked.

I had no problem with Rhonda meeting my family. She'd forgive me for them. I thought about

showing her the basement.  But I knew I couldn't
explain the lack of heat and water and she'd think I
was lying about living down there.  She'd press all
the more to see the inside of the house.  There was
nothing I could do.  Rhonda could never, ever see
where I lived.  She could never know the real me.
If the place where you sleep really tells the story of
the person, then I was a horror story.  I was a
gruesome tale that could neither be enjoyed nor
understood.  That person was too grotesque even for
me to think about.  Thank God the human psyche
blocks, forgets and rationalizes the most irrational
and appalling truths.

Christy Hillshire's unsolicited and illicit
invasion provided my only recollection of a girl
ever being at the creek.  All the others had only
been to the Chicken Ranch, and that was just a
decrepit old building, not the creek.  You can't even
see the water from there.  I knew Rhonda was
special and I knew she had to go.  She wanted to
know me, to glimpse at something other than my
ragged exterior, to see my space.  I knew what I had
to do.  I had to take her to the creek and dispose of
her.

## Chapter 16

A small grass fire in our yard illuminated the night. The greater surprise came as Duke stood in the yard, watching it burn.

"What are you doing here?" I asked, happily.

"Escaped," is all he said.

"Do you want me to get the water hose and put out the fire?" I asked my brother.

"Aw, hell no! Let it burn. That's the best way to get rid of the evidence." By that I knew Duke meant to let the whole house burn down. I wanted to change out of my sweat soaked shirt from my run home. I would have settled for at least warming myself by the fire. Duke told me to stay away from the house. Like always, I did what he said, no matter how uncomfortable it made me. We took a seat on the retaining wall in the neighbor's yard and watched the flames twist and turn across the lawn. The orange and amber flames danced a sultry tango, burning a path to the house.

"Where's mama?" I asked.

"I don't know, but she's not in the house," Duke said. "I checked."

I didn't altogether believe him. He and our mama didn't get along all too well. Duke blamed mama for his problems. More than that, he blamed her for sending him away to all the different homes and hospitals.

"How do you keep getting out of wherever you are?"

"They can't hold me," he said. "Ain't nothing wrong with me. I don't need to be locked up."

"I think it's kinda cool that you keep cutting loose."

"Boy, there ain't nothing cool about it," Duke said categorically.

"I think it would be cool to be with you. So, I've been getting into trouble at school, hoping they'd send me off like they did to you."
Something akin to rage, but far worse ran across my brother's face.

"The boys they put me up with are crazy. You hear me! Those fuckers are stone cold crazy. You don't know what you're talking about," Duke leaped from the wall and screamed in my face. Shivers ran through me. I didn't know if it was because I was sitting around in a wet shirt or if fear caused my body to quake.

"You'd be there to protect me," I said, wrapping my arms around my chest. This served both as a measure of self-protection from Duke and the chill in the air.

"That's where you're wrong, Fat Boy. I'll kill you before I let you go through my misery. I mean it," Duke howled. "Do you hear me? I will kill you and mama, too, if she tries to send you away," he said with balled fists.

His face became liquid. I could see the blood pumping as his veins started to swell and sweat beaded across his brow. The conviction and ferocity in his voice let me know that he meant every word he said. I felt sure I had earned a beating.

"What have you been doing at school, huh?" he demanded.

"I give the teachers a hard time here and there and I've been in a few fights."

"So what did they do about it?" he asked.

"They called mama and I went to the principal's office and stood with my nose in the corner and held dictionaries in bold hands." I extended my arms to demonstrate.

"Is that all?" he demanded.

"I had to take all these tests and answer a bunch of questions about shapes and stupid spots on cards," I continued. "I must have failed 'cause I go to the little special classes for most of the day in school."

Honesty didn't serve me well. "Listen, you little dumb ass. And I mean listen good. If you think this messed up house is bad, you can't even imagine the torture I go through in these hospitals and group homes. Straighten up or else, and don't ever even talk to me about it again." He poked his finger in the corner of my lip pushing my head back as he emphasized, "Ever!"

I think Duke was about to pound me into a pool of blood and pulp. My savior came via rushing emergency vehicles. Some do gooder had phoned the fire department and two large trucks arrived to extinguish the flaming eraser that might have cleaned our slate in life. It took the firemen all of two minutes to soak the ground. In two more minutes they drove away. Duke and I sat back down on the wall in silence. I wondered how the fire started. Though I was afraid to ask, I felt certain my brother probably had tried to add arson to his list of criminal activities.

## Chapter 17

Rhonda and I walked down the well-worn path along Carp Bridge. I tried not to talk too much as we made our way. As we ambled I noticed an oversized green and yellow garden spider just under the edge of the bridge. I glared at it and then glanced back at Rhonda. I knew I couldn't go ballistic on the spider, not in front of her. Just seeing the creature caused the hair to rise on my neck and bumps to well up all over my body. I clinched my fists, and willed the spider to understand that I'd be back for it later. I gritted my teeth.

"Are you okay?" Rhonda asked, breaking my trance.

"It's just the spider there. I hate spiders. Ordinarily I kill them," I said, holding in my vehemence.

"Stop it. I'm surprised," she said. "I don't know this side of you. You let that spider alone. Spiders are good for the ecosystem. They eat insects."

Just then the spider moved along its web. I lost control. I snapped off a branch and knocked the arachnid to the ground and then proceeded to grind it into oblivion.

"For the love of God, stop it!" Rhonda screamed. I had never heard her raise her voice prior to that moment. It didn't suit her. As for me, I had known awkwardness in the past. This was something new. I could hear my own heavy breathing. I tried to think, to gain focus. I wanted to explain. Instead, I did what my family does best. I held my tongue.

After a spell, in a calming voice, Rhonda said, "So this is your creek." That was her way. She found the good in everything.

"Well, it's not mine, but I feel like it is. I love it here. I come all the time. When we were kids we splashed in the water to cool off in the hot summers. Then we started fishing here, and finally just hanging out. You know, guy stuff."

"No, I can't say I know too much about guy stuff, but it sounds like you've had a lot of good times here," she said.

"This place is my window on the world. Once we found a snake skin as long as my arm span." I spread my arms wide. "Another time we saw this thing that looked like a cross between a bear and a dog. It moved on all fours and swam under water."

"That's a beaver, silly," Rhonda instructed.

"Ah...That makes sense. For years we thought..." I paused. "Aw, you don't even want to know. Time to time we've spotted blue herons here," I said with glee.

"How long have you been coming here?" she asked.

"A long time. My brother used to come here. He showed it to me," I said, proudly.

"That's cool."

"Yeah, it's the best thing he ever did for me," I said.

"You really do love it here, don't you?" she asked.

"Yes. The creek turned from a place for fun and pleasure to a place of safety for me," I paused and looked at the beauty of it all. Rhonda added to it. I continued, "I love to come here to just sit by the creek and take a load off my mind. I think

about the zany days of my life. Sometimes I come
here and do nothing but watch the water flow. Even
after storms, the water swells and moves so
peacefully and gracefully. I let the creek take all
my worries and the madness of my home life away
and it washes me clean."

"It sounds like this place is your sanctuary,"
Rhonda stated.

"I never thought of it that way, but I guess it
is." I held my chin to indicate deep thought. "I do.
I treat it sort of like the altar call at church; I turn
over the problems and the uncertainties of my life to
the creek. It takes them all away," I said.

"That's powerful. Do you have a favorite
part of the creek?" Rhonda asked.

"Yeah…" I stammered a bit. "This is it.
I've never been to the ocean. So this one little
sandy area is as close to the beach as I know. I
hope I get to see the ocean some day. I bet it would
be a great place to go and just hang out."

"Oh, you must see the ocean. Where the
water meets the horizon is a sight to see. The beach
at the ocean is bigger and the sand is whiter. The
problem is the ocean beach has jellyfish and they're
gross. One stung my father when I was a little girl.
I don't care for them."

"That's the same way I feel about spiders."
Rhonda smiled at me and spun in a couple of
circles. She often did odd things like that.

"I don't kill jellyfish," she said, while
tracing my footprints in the sand. We both laughed.
"Thanks for bringing me here. I think your special
place is definitely beautiful." God, she was the
best. I wanted to abandon my plan and hold her
there, to keep her with me for as long as I lived.

"So tell me, what else are you afraid of, other than spiders?" Rhonda asked.

"I'm not afraid of spiders!" I insisted. "I don't like them." She smiled a knowing smile.

"Sometimes I think about nuclear war. I'm afraid we are going to get into some silly political argument with Russia and then both countries will press the buttons," Rhonda confessed.

"Do really believe the Russians would do that? Can they hate us that much?" I asked.

"That's all anybody ever says. All the books and movies want us to believe that the Russians are mean and evil and that they hate us," she said.

"And that scares you?"

"No, nuclear war scares me," she said emphatically.

"They won't blow up the planet just 'cause they don't like each other."

"Look at what you did to that spider just because you don't like them," Rhonda said.

Years of spider destruction flashed through my mind. I didn't feel sorry for the spiders. I felt ashamed of my rage and how I couldn't control it. I wondered how much I was like my brother. Maybe I'd get my wish and get shipped off to some institution just like him if I kept messing around.

Rhonda lightly tapped a finger on my forehead. "Are you still in there?"

"Yeah. It's just a lot to think about. You know, nuclear war and all."

"Boy, do I know. I think about it all the time. I constantly beg my father to build a bomb shelter. I know it won't save us, but it might make me sleep better," she said.

"Wow, I love you." I announced. "I have trouble sleeping, too. I think about spiders and other stuff."

"Do you ever think about the end of the world?"

"Uh huh, but I think about what it will be like when Jesus comes."

"What?" Rhonda looked sincerely puzzled.

"I worry about the end of days. Our preacher says the hour is close at hand. And there's this picture at church. It's right at the front door. It shows everybody dying and going to heaven or hell. It's an awful sight." I started to ask her if she died today where she would go, but I didn't. My Rhonda was goodness. She embodied all the purity and innocence this world has to offer. She had to be saved. God surely wanted her in heaven.

"We think about deep stuff for a couple of kids," Rhonda said

I gripped her hand. I felt the moisture evaporate right out of my throat and make its way to my palms and forehead. I knew it looked weird to be sweating on a breezy fall day. I bet we stood there for a good twenty minutes before I said a word. My mind raced. I felt uneasy with how much I had told her about spiders and Jesus. Yet, I felt warm and…and safe talking with her. Rhonda was so strong, so smart and so everything. That's all I could articulate. She was everything. Everything I needed.

"Listen, babe, my house is sort of gross and I really don't want to show it to you. Besides, my mom has a strict rule that we never have company."

"That's okay," she said. I blew a deep sigh of relief until she continued. "I want to meet her, too. I can wait and see your room when your mother is at home."

"I don't even sleep in the house. I stay in the basement," I told her.

"Don't be silly. There's no rush. I know you are a private person. It didn't take me long to figure that out about you. You can show me when you feel comfortable with it."

I twisted inside and out with anxiety. "No, you don't understand. No one ever goes in our house."

"I don't care what your house looks like. I just want to be where you live," she said. I didn't doubt her sincerity, but she left me with no choice. I brought her to the creek and it was wonderful, but I knew now more than ever that this had to end.

I surveyed her. Her natural beauty captivated me. Unlike girls our age, Rhonda didn't wear an ounce of makeup. She didn't color, tease or spray her hair. What you saw was what you got. For a punk like me, she was a treasure beyond belief. And just like everything else in my life, I planned to sabotage it.

"Babe, there's something I've got to say. I need you to let me get it all out before you say anything." I went on to lay out the old 'it's not you, it's me' crappy crap. I tried to be sincere, poetic and not to quote every line from *Freebird*.

When I finished, she spoke immediately. "You brought me here to break up with me?" Rhonda demanded, and pulled away from me. I looked at her. I didn't know what the right thing was to say in response. So, I said nothing. No surprise.

"I love you for bringing me to your special place. I bet you've never brought any other girl here with you."

I nodded.

"You do what you have to do. You work through it. I know you love me. I'll wait for you." We kissed for a long time. We parted lips, but held close enough that I could feel her barely breathing as she said, "If it turns out that you never come back to me, promise me something," she paused. I had to agree before I even heard what she wanted. So I nodded.

"No. Say you promise," Rhonda instructed.

I relented and said "yes" obediently.

"Promise me that you will do noble things."

I smiled and whispered, "Yes." We kissed a sweet and bitter kiss one last time.

As I walked her home I thought about my promise to her. I wondered what it meant to do noble things. Did that mean I shouldn't kill any more spiders? I felt it too soon to even consider promises that I might break. Instead, I thought how lucky I'd been to ever even know a girl like Rhonda. Afterwards, my actions belied a guy who had just dispatched the love of his life. I sang songs that reminded me of Rhonda as I sprinted home. I can't remember ever being so happy when I headed to the house. My euphoria continued when I arrived home.

# Winter

## Chapter 18

Busted! I didn't finish a project for school,
so I decided to stay home and avoid humiliation.
The day lingered and grew colder rather than
warmer. I held up in the confines of the basement.
I ran two space heaters and took in classics on
television. I watched *F-Troop, I Dream of Jeannie,
Gilligan's Island, McHale's Navy, I Love Lucy,* and
*Mr. Ed* before I finally got to work on the overdue
project. I worked like a madman and actually made
great progress. I knew tardy papers lost a letter
grade, but the end product turned out okay and I felt
good about it. Long about the time I normally
arrived home from school, I called my mom to
check in with her.

"I've been worried to death about you,"
Mama growled through the phone.

"Why?" I asked. That turned out to be a big
mistake and strike one.

"Because of the snow jam! Why didn't you
call me as soon as you got out of school?"

"I am."

I had a vineyard of extension cords snaked
through the basement; however, my hacked in
phone line would not reach the door. I couldn't
look out to see what mama was going on about. All
I could think of was snow. I stuttered and
stammered. Strike two.

"I can't believe it took you this long to walk
home. School has been out for hours." My silence
proved to be strike three.

"You don't even know the whole damn city is covered with snow," she said more than asked. I answered with more silence.

"You had me scared to no end. I waited to hear from you and now because of you, I'm stuck. I can't get home in this mess. I'll have to stay here overnight. Little mister, we're gonna have a come to Jesus when I get to the house." She stopped speaking.

Snow in Atlanta led to a mad rush in the grocery stores. People cleared the shelves of bread, milk and other staples. Inclement weather shut down the southern city as we were ill prepared to clear the roads or drive on slippery thoroughfares.

I knew mama's scolding was far from finished. A second later she carried on, "Why did you lay out of school? Never mind, I want you to see if you can you stay at a friend's house. Call me and let me know where you are. You'd better not tarry."

"Okay, lighten up, will ya?"

"Don't talk. Listen. Let the water drip in all the faucets before you leave," she admonished.

"Yeah, whatever."

"Don't sass me, boy. You hear me?"

"Yes, ma'am," I said meekly.

The snow psyched me so. I immediately ran out to take part in a wintertime rarity for the south. The mini-blizzard left the waters of the creek flowing slowly and absolutely beautifully. Silo, MD, Bubba and I did some dumpster diving and found cardboard boxes behind the golf clubhouse. On it we slid, rolled and slipped up and down on the winter wonderland of the golf course. We had snowball fights, and threw snowballs at cars like we had done with eggs so long ago. What a blast. We

were soaked inside and out.  Once we started the
trek home I felt certain our sweat-drenched clothes
would surely lead to hypothermia this time.

      The snow didn't melt as expected.  It
snowed more and stuck.  My mom spent three
nights sleeping on the floor of her office.  I stayed
home the first night, but abandoned the drafty old
house for the other two.  It felt like a miracle to
have three days with cancelled classes.  Bubba, Silo
and I camped out in MD's basement.  We had a
great time.

      When I finally got around to going home I
found the pipes had been frozen.  I forgot to leave
them dripping like mama said.  Once I had
discovered the snow I never thought about her
admonition again.  I hated the house so, and with no
water in the basement it just hadn't crossed my
mind.  I freaked.  Mama still had to deal with the
school skipping business, and now I had let the
pipes freeze and burst.  She was going to kill me for
sure.  I knew I had to call her.  I decided to make
the call and then after we talked I'd run away,
maybe for good.

## Chapter 19

"I told you to run the water before you left," my mama screamed across the phone line.

"I never went upstairs into the house. I didn't think I needed to let it drip. You see the pipes run across the ceiling and I had the space heaters on in the basement the whole time. I thought that would do the trick," I explained.

Of course the pipe that busted was in the dirt room. The space heater had no affect in there and now the room was ice coated. Oddly, it looked beautiful. Opaque ice crystals lined the floor, walls and dangled from the rusted water pipes. They glistened like diamonds and alabaster, a natural wonder.

"My God, boy! Are you trying to burn the house down?" Mama howled.

"But...but I thought. I was just trying to keep the pipes warm."

"I told you not to run those damn heaters. They're fire hazards..."

"How am I supposed to stay warm?" I whimpered.

"Hush your mouth, boy. I've got to figure out how on Earth we're going to deal with this. Don't you know I can't afford a plumber? Even if I had a red cent to my name, how are we supposed to let someone come in the house? Did you ever think about that?"

"I'll clean all the junk out of the house. It won't take but a couple of weeks or so," I said.

"Just shut up! You've done enough already. Go get a water key from Mr. Miles and turn off the water before any more damage is done."

"But Mama..."

"Don't but me, boy," she said harshly. "I'll deal with you shortly. I'm coming home. The roads should be clear enough by now."

I had no idea how to turn off the water, much less where to even begin. So, rather than doing what mama said, I hurried across the street and asked a neighbor for help. I showed him the icy art created by the busted pipes in the dirt room. He seemed distracted and looked around the basement. He asked a bunch of questions about my lair and the whereabouts of my mom. I proudly answered questions about the only presentable section of our house. I thought it wasn't that bad down there.

He didn't do anything to help. He invited me to his house and became very weird when I refused. I realized how peculiar my situation looked. I had to get out of there and on the double. I just up and ran. I went back to MD's house. His parents were brawling. I could hear them fussing from the carport. So I kept on and went to the only safe place I could think of to get out of the snow and hide from the storm my mom would be bringing down on me.

## Chapter 20

Flowing unhampered, the waters of the creek glistened in the moonlight. Snowflakes sparkled like the stars that shone on the face of the water. Snow drifts piled up on the slopes all around the creek. A cardinal perched on a leafless tree sat in contrast to the field of white that coated the landscape. The golf course looked like a winter wonderland as I trudged across it to the Chicken Ranch.

Restless as ever, I sat in a dark corner. I never really found it easy to sleep. My intense fear of the awesome speed of spiders plagued me. Added to that, living in the primitiveness of the basement I developed an intense dislike of cold weather, which over time had come to include cool and moderate temperatures as well. I couldn't decide which had more impact. I ran space heaters all the time. The vibrating of the metal coils served me like white noise. I needed it for what little sleep I managed. As a consequence I ran the aluminum fire hazards, as mama called them, all year long.

Even though we had threadbare blankets, candles and foam mats in the Chicken Ranch, I feared freezing to death in the cold, dark building. So I built a fire. I lay watching the flames and embers. The crackling adequately replaced my much needed background noise of the space heaters. I calmed and thought back about all the great times I had at the creek and in the Chicken Ranch. I recalled my tender Rhonda. I dwelled on her, immortalizing her and our time together.

## Chapter 21

"34 to Dispatch. We have a visual. There's smoke coming from an abandoned building. Probably vagrants.

"Dispatch to 34. Copy that. A police unit is in route to assist."

The radio chatter cut through the frosty night.

"What the…" I groaned. As the fog in my head lifted I recognized my surroundings. I gained enough clarity to realize the sirens, radios and crunching snow were not part of an elaborate dream. Time to run, again.

I shot out of the Chicken Ranch and ran wide open. Enough already, I thought. I decided to go on home and take my stripes. I think I set a record getting to the house from the creek. I didn't want to be out in the cold for a second longer than necessary.

As I arrived at the house, blue lights illuminated the night and reflected off the powdery white landscape. Fear ripped through me. My mom? She must have had an accident driving in the snow. She wouldn't have been out if it weren't for me. What had I caused now? My mind raced.

Another possibility was my brother had escaped again or he had really hurt somebody this time. I took off thrashing through the snow. I got close and saw the gaggle of police and others in front of my house. I saw a news truck hoisting its antenna. Then I stopped. That seemed odd. Duke must have finally snapped and actually killed someone.

An officer noticed me as I stood staring into the carnival of activity. Our eyes met and my world

collapsed. Like the few seconds, less than a
heartbeat, when that initial spider moved across my
face, I knew this moment in time would alter the
course of my life. I turned and ran. Somehow I
didn't run fast enough. In the past I had always
outran or outsmarted my pursuers. I had done so
not a half an hour ago when I escaped the
firefighters at the Chicken Ranch.

I think I was tired. Tired from lack of sleep.
Tired of running. Tired of lying. Tired of hiding.
Just tired.

I found myself ensconced in the back seat of
a pale blue Ford Granada. No one treated me like a
criminal. I didn't understand. Cops and women in
plain clothes talked to me in whispered voices.
They kept asking if I needed anything and used the
word victim an awful lot. I saw my mom's car.
She had made it home in the snow. When I asked
for her, I was told not to worry, I'd be safe. For a
while I wondered what was happening to her.
Finally, I saw mama being escorted to a police
cruiser in handcuffs.

I began crying and screaming, "She's not a
criminal. Let her go. That's my mama!" I kept
saying the same thing over and over and could not
be consoled. A very nice black cop and an officer
of the court, whatever that is, got in the front seat,
started the car and slowly began to navigate through
the crowd.

I slammed myself against the window as we
drove past the house. I saw camera crews and other
people going inside the house. That was wrong.
They can't see that. They can't see us. They can't
see me. Then, I began to feel like a victim. I felt
violated. I felt exposed. Before even devising a

plan, I had kicked the window out of the Ford
Granada and took off running.

## Chapter 22

Somewhat dazed, I tended to my blood scraped arms in MD's basement. I held up there for days. While in the hideaway some of my buddies came to see me. A couple of guys even camped out with me. All the kids seemed to know where I was hiding. Some of my so-called friends came over to rag me about the house after they saw it on the TV news. They said I was going to be sent to Milledgeville with my brother. Under any other circumstances I would have stomped their asses into the ground. Good that I didn't. After all their lip, none of them dropped a dime on me. I stayed safe for six nights in MD's basement.

One afternoon the basement door opened unexpectedly. MD should have been in school. It wasn't a dream this time. My nightmare had come true. The police, social workers and the officer of the court all piled into the tiny cement room. I had no way out.

I quickly learned MD's dad turned me in to the cops. He stood behind the group that stormed his basement to take me into custody.

"I'm sorry son, but I don't need this mess around my house," he said by way of explanation.

Dog-eat-dog mentality never has made sense to me. I detest the way people turn on each other. In my neighborhood we were all poor. We had lived in the same couple of blocks forever. Solidarity should have ruled our every day. No matter what personal gain or fear of personal loss caused people to turn on their own kind. As long as I live I may never understand this phenomenon. It's a *bona fide* mystery to me.

Even more astounding I have always found it incomprehensible how nature can readily and thoroughly wreak havoc on itself. Storms, droughts, etcetera add true meaning to natural disasters. In my thinking, those two words should be mutually exclusive. If Pastor Frank was right, then nature got help from us sinners in bringing on the wrath of God. In a messed up way that was cause and effect that I could understand. I couldn't swallow, however, the selfishness of simply mistreating your own kind.

I fidgeted in the back seat while blaming and cursing myself. I knew Pastor Frank was right about me all along. My sin was the root of all my problems. I wondered if I'd ever see the house again. I hoped not. Would I ever see my mama again? Good or bad, she was my mother. I prayed that God would have mercy on her. After that, I begged Jesus to help me.

Divine providence. My Redeemer sent a sign, a familiar sign. This sign came in white letters on a green metal background. It read *Peachtree Creek*. Many signs denoted its proper name, but I rarely heard it used. We simply and affectionately called it, *the creek*. In reality, Peachtree Creek seemed more like a little river than a creek, as the waters only provided a couple of places to cross easily. My beloved creek flowed into the Chattahoochee, Atlanta's main river.

The creek brought years of discovery for me. My horizons broadened as I saw many things there that I had never seen before. I made discoveries in those waters like the snake skin, the beaver, a blue heron, the Chicken Ranch, friendships, and the touch of a girl. I grew up with the tall brittle Georgia pines, dogwoods, sand, silt, red clay and kudzu of the creek.

I likened the creek to Howard Carter's 1922 unearthing of Tutankhamen's tomb. Among all the treasures there, lies a curse. I knew all too well that a sacred place doesn't ensure all visitors will act nobly. Many of the worst things in the world happen in Jerusalem, a city holy to all of the children of Abraham and ground hallowed to most of the world's faithful.

Regardless of what happened, nothing ever compromised the creek. It survived tornadoes, floods, ice, snow and more, only to morph into something better and more wondrous than before. No matter what nature threw at it--the bends of the creek, its obstacles, twists, and turns--the waters continued to move. The creek itself provided a life lesson for me. I learned that what life does to me is not as important as how I respond. On a deep level I understood that in the course of the evening my life would change, forever. I wondered if I'd respond to the changes as majestically as the creek did. I wondered if I was capable of flowing so nobly. The thought made me smile just as the Ford Granada crossed Carp Bridge.

Life as Fat Boy knew it had ended.

# Encounters
## Chapter 23

"First of all I need to hear from you so I can get to know you a little better. I have a journal I'll give you at the end of our time today. I want you to write in it regularly. You do not have to do it daily. The important thing is I need you to write important things in the journal as they happen. By that I mean things that are important to you. I'm not so much looking for what you had for lunch as much as things that happened that caused you to feel excited, anxious, thrilled, nervous, irritated or happy. Okay?" she said, without waiting for me to take a seat.

Dr. Andrea Hayes had long worked for the state social services office. Of late she had turned to private practice, but still contracted with the juvenile court. She had a reputation for handling severe cases, the kind that got outsourced due the nature of the crime or the hostility of the patient. This was not the case here. Quite the contrary, she had asked to have this one.

"I'm not big into writing and I'm not the type of guy who goes around thinking oh, when that happens it makes me feel anxious. You know what I mean?" I offered little to no help or cooperation with Dr. Hayes' questions. I resented my predicament and acted it out.

"At your age, you may not be as keenly aware of your feelings as an adult, but they are there at the conscious and subconscious level. What I need you to do is to begin to be mindful of that. The journal will help you to focus on and understand those feelings."

Dr. Hayes stood close to five feet six inches tall, or so I guessed from the few seconds I had seen her standing. She had met me at the door of her office and promptly took a seat. Her shoulder length black hair glistened in the light of the waiting room like polished onyx. Her apparel and demeanor matched the fastidious room. The polished space had an organized flow to it. The office was open, well lit and had the absence of clutter. Her desk held only a pad, a pen holder and a blotter. Crystal eyes peered from behind her professional yet popular narrow glasses. She was a sight to behold in her own right. I openly stared at the attractive young psychologist. All I could think about was how youthful she looked. I couldn't get a read on her age. I thought her the Doogie Howser of the counseling profession.

"Mindful. Right," I said sarcastically. Dr. Hayes dropped her eyes and took notes. That made me anxious. "It's not like I'm trying to be a hard case. I know I have to be here and that you can say I'm being uncooperative and then I'm screwed. It's just...well, my mom taught us never to talk about our lives, especially the house," I said by means of explanation.

"I hear you. You're correct; my report does have some impact on your treatment program. I don't know what being *screwed* means to you, but you can't be taken out of your home again. Do you know that?" Dr. Hayes asked.

I shrugged my shoulders.

"It's a fact. You are in a healthy home. The Carpenters legally adopted you. You are safe. You're safe here, too. Everything you say is confidential."

"What about your report?" I asked, focusing on her legal pad.

"My report simply notes your progress. It does not reveal any of the information you share with me," she said, focusing on the legal pad and the very sharp pencil she held in her hand.

"I know you're uneasy with all of this. So to start off, will you tell me about your adopted parents?" Dr. Hayes asked.

"Why? You know them already. You knew them before I did."

"Yes, I've met them. I know Dr. Carpenter professionally. I want to know how you perceive them. How are you finding your new life?"

"I feel like an imposter," I said.

"Why is that?" she asked.

"All that they do is alien to me. Don't get me wrong. They have been good to me, but I just don't get them."

"Can you give me a specific example?" Dr. Hayes asked.

"One of the first things Mrs. Carpenter told me was that she is Jewish and Dr. Carpenter converted to her religion."

"Is that a problem for you?"

"Not except for how shocked I was to hear her say it. It made me feel stupid," I admitted.

"Why did she make you feel stupid?"

"It's really embarrassing," I stopped and screwed myself deeper into the sofa.

"You don't have to tell me. I want you to be comfortable talking at all times," Dr. Hayes said warmly.

"It's well…I never met a Jewish person before," I said. "My world view was so limited that I thought the Jews were historical people from the

Bible and not around anymore. That's how Pastor Frank talked about them. He made out like all the Jews were dead or had become Christians, now."

Dr. Hayes took a moment to respond as she made a few notes on her intrusive legal pad. "That's nothing to be ashamed of at all," she finally said without slowing down her rapidly moving writing hand. "Especially, since someone you respected taught you that. You had every reason to believe what he said was true. Of course, you are now aware that the Jewish people and faith is very much alive as well as many other religions?"

"Yes, I get that now," I said trying to determine if I ever really respected Pastor Frank and what else he had said that fell short of the truth.

"Have you explored the Carpenters' religion with them?" she asked.

"No, I'm not ready," I said. "I don't know if I ever will be. Not to mention I still fell pretty stupid about the whole thing." I wondered if I'd ever believe another thing anyone had to say from a pulpit.

"Are there other things that make you feel awkward about your new family?" Dr. Hayes asked.

"I guess so. It's like we are opposites. I was raised on fried foods. The Carpenters are health oriented. More than that, they eat stuff I've never even heard of before like gazpacho, basmati rice and gnocchi. They like to take family walks after dinner. Their house is filled with books, not fluff, serious literature and nonfiction. Both of them are very intelligent."

"It sounds like a very different place than you are from, for sure. How about the Carpenters? Do you get along with them?" Dr. Hayes asked.

"Yeah, sure. They're easygoing people. I like them."

"Do you like your new life with them?"

"They have a good life, but the goofy thing is that they're hurting. They have some overwhelming sense of guilt for having access to the good things in life. I tried to break them of that and tell them it's better on their side of the fence. I think they hoped to make up for it by adopting my poor ass," I said.

"How's that working for them?"

I wanted to laugh at that question. I looked beyond Dr. Hayes and focused on a bookshelf. It only took a few seconds to gather my composure. I answered, "My messed up story's not enough to fill in that big gaping hole in their lives."

"You're a young guy for all this psychological theorizing you are doing," Dr. Hayes said, while jotting notes with her super sharp pencil.

"Time to time I pay attention to what's going on around me. I got better at that thanks to the Carpenters. Before, when I lived with my mama, I had to monitor and control every conversation. Add to that my brother has been through every kind of treatment imaginable, and I had that awful stint in the group home. As you know, I live with two professional therapists and this fine county requires that I see you twice a week. I think I'm ready to take my orals and defend a dissertation in psychology."

"You are an interesting character. Let's get back to your parents. What else can you tell me?"

"They are environmentally sensitive."

Dr. Hayes interrupted me. "You have told me a lot about them, but not how you relate to them."

"The Carpenters have an open policy. It makes me queasy. I don't like to talk about most things. My taboo list reads like a phone book. They don't censure anything. I find conversation at dinner to be too mature for my liking."

"What sort of mature topics do they discuss?" she asked.

I knew she was going to ask that. "Mrs. Carpenter has no filter for discussing her…her female stuff. And Dr. Carpenter will talk about sexual dysfunctions he read about at the office."

"I'll give you that one. I can see where a young man would shy away from those topics. Do you ever refer to them as mom and dad?" asked Dr. Hayes.

"No, I call them by their first names when we're together. I call them Dr. or Mrs. Carpenter when I'm talking about them to other people."

"I understand your theory on why they adopted you. Does that bother you?"

"No. Not really. I've learned a lot from them. The Carpenters bring their work home. They are consumed with psychotherapy, Reki, yoga, martial arts and mind over body inner strength stuff. I've learned about body language and self-discipline. I can focus and listen to people ramble and hear the real source of the conversation. They've helped me to develop an understanding of cultural differences between my old house and neighborhood and where I live with them. I have learned how to pick up on subtle statements people make, whether they say it out loud or not."

Dr. Hayes looked doubtful. "I'm not sure I know what you are trying to say."

"You know, people make statements about themselves with their clothes, watches, shoes, cars and whatnot. All those things are the props in a story a person wants to tell. Sometimes they are projecting and other times they are concealing. But it's there. I'm like a kid with Autism. All the information of a person is like sensory overload for me most of the time. I hear it, collect it and then analyze it. Just to get it out of my head I do an instant read. On occasion, my head is all muddied with the junk going on in my life and to get a read on someone takes a bit. I have to hear them talk. Funny, folks who have suffered and are suffering carry it on them like a scent. I mean it. I can actually smell their vulnerability. It's like a predator smelling the blood on wounded prey."

"Sounds like you really are an attentive listener. Good for you. Have your parents ever done anything that terribly upset you?" Dr. Hayes asked.

I thought for a second and answered, "Yeah, they bought me a car."

"Most people beg their parents to buy a vehicle for them. Why is that so bad?"

"I'm not into getting gifts. We never had anything given to us. I earn what's mine. I always have and I always will," I said boastfully.

"Did you let the Carpenters know that getting the car as a gift upset you?"

"They figured it out pretty quick. I blew a gasket. They solved the problem by letting me pay them back for the car. I give them money from my paycheck every two weeks. I feel pretty sure they are depositing it in a savings account for me. I think they find my earnest efforts cute. That pisses me off. Is that relating to them?" I quipped.

"I know it's not easy bringing up hurtful topics and you've already made it clear that you're too smart for that sort of juvenile talk," she said.

Bam. She nailed me. I felt like I should apologize. I didn't. I did what I knew she wanted. I kept talking. "Dr. Carpenter is all in to preparedness. He all but made me join the Boy Scouts. I couldn't even think about driving the car until we went over every item in the emergency bag he purchased and placed in the trunk. We unpacked the jumper cables, roadside flares, a blanket, a flashlight and a tiny AM radio, the whole kit. As part of the deal I had to check the batteries in the radio when the time changes twice a year and replace them if necessary," I said while making air quotes over the last four words.

"Some situation will come up and you'll thank him for teaching you to be prepared."

"I already appreciate what he has done for me. I'm grateful to both of them, and I don't really care about their reasons. I get it that the two of them have sacrificed for me."

## Chapter 24

I really find it hard to write in this journal. It's unnatural. In fact, it's a pain in my ass. I've had this thing sitting by my bed for more than a month and I haven't written a word before tonight. I wouldn't write anything if it weren't part of my state mandated treatment. My guess is sooner or later Dr. Hayes or somebody will ask to see it. I hope a stream of consciousness counts as a "meaningful entry." As much as I hate it, I know I have to play by the rules to stay out of a group home or institution, no matter what Dr. Hayes says about my adoption being permanent.

Boy, was Duke right about not wanting me to end up in one of those places. I don't get it why he kept doing stupid shit and getting sent back. That's a mess I never want around the house, again. My short stint in a group home took me to the edge. In that horrible place I acted out my aggression and landed in this messed up treatment program.

I'm supposed to treat this journal like a diary. Dr. Hayes says that I can share my secrets here. I know that my secrets are not necessarily safe in this journal. Dr. Hayes and any other people who may or may not read this have to know that I'm aware of that as I write. They may not know that this journaling stuff is hard to get my head around. I doubt they care. I have a mixture of emotions about writing this crap. Part of me fears that if I am too honest someone else might read it and find out what I really am. On the other hand, I sort of want to put it all out there and hope someone will read it. Maybe then I can be understood. Maybe then I can get out of this cluster fuck situation. I know that's not happening. So, I have to be careful, because my stuff is way too messed up to write.  In either case people won't believe my life story could be true and I don't really want to open the door to my fortress.  I worked too hard to build this wall and moat to protect myself.  I've grown to appreciate its safety and I understand it doubles as my self-destructive prison.

Dr. Hayes and Dr. Carpenter say the writing is for me.  I already know how I feel.  I know every little bit of it.  I don't know why I have to write it all down and then go and say it all again with Dr. Hayes.  What's the point of doing the same thing over and over?  It's not like I'm going say one thing here and something different with Dr. Hayes.  It's all the same.  I mean, I'm fairly happy.  I mind my own business.  I try to keep attention off of me.  So what if occasionally the plates in my head get rubbed the wrong way and I fume like a volcano?

In any event, nothing of interest happened to me today and I can't think of a thing that is weighing heavy on my mind.  I figure since Dr. Hayes has asked about my mom and the Carpenters, sooner or later she'll get around to asking about the group home.  So, I'll save her the trouble.  This may just work out great.  When she does ask maybe I'll just hand her the journal and be in for an easy session.  Right, like that'll work.

Let's see, where do I start?  Okay, how about this?  The brain surgeons who dragged me out of MD's basement entered me into the foster home parade.  I managed to raise enough hell to get adjudicated.  My next stop came at the group home.  In that rat trap I finally learned to live in a dog eat dog world.  The group home was a lesson in preparedness, rigor and strategy.  Power and safety came in numbers.  Gangs vied for supremacy.  I tried to help the newcomers and outsiders, but mostly I had to help myself.

Self-preservation was how I adapted to the dog eat dog world. This one demonic gang banger, who called himself Eggie Baby, came for me every day. Each time he brought a new weapon or a friend to help his cause. He had no idea of my internal turmoil. He had chosen his mark poorly. Coming for me while I was so filled with anger was like plunging a bleeding hand into a tank of starving piranhas. I beat Eggie Baby worse each time he'd run up on me. That's in large part why he kept coming. He didn't understand losing. I considered lying down and taking a few licks, but I knew that would make it worse. Then, I'd be his boy. That wasn't an option.

All of those guys in that place were touched. I mean I know I wasn't there without reason, but these fellows came from severely torn up families. Their parents and family members did unimaginable things to them, leaving these boys violently insane. Just being locked up together took its toll on all of us. The counselors said that on "Day One, Level One" you would come in as one person and at the end of your time you'd leave as another. That happened to one and all, but had nothing in the world to do with the treatment program. The place itself, the people locked inside, that's what changed us.

The treatment program had five levels. Day One, Level One consisted of living in solitary for three days and nights. At this level you had to have your head shaved. They dressed you in medical scrubs and put plastic bags over your feet. If you were quiet and did as you were told, then the next step came in the sweet liberty of seven days of

wearing wrist and ankle straps. At this level we
were escorted everywhere, even into the stall of the
bathroom. Next you could move about freely
without an escort, but you still were bound. The
straps graduated to shackles which allowed you to
eat, brush your teeth and shuffle about. The hat
trick was not to get killed in this vulnerable time.

Any outburst, fights, cussing or anything got
you busted back down. The director took a hard
core position. You didn't get knocked back down
just one level. It was all the way back down to Day
One, Level One. You had to get the haircut and
everything all over again. Some dudes rarely ever
saw the light of day. When they said all their
clients would change, they meant it. It was a fact,
but the metamorphosis was not necessarily, if ever,
for the better. I had to tap my own rage to get
along, to survive.

Very few of us made it to level five where
we could wear street clothes and go to classes.
Most of us lost hope. We all lost something in that
place. Many of the other boys' folks were dead or
strung out on junk. I gave a beating to this one boy
who spit in my food. About a week later his father
came for visitation and thanked me. I mean, what
kind of shit is that? In my short stay in that torture
chamber, two of the other guys committed suicide.
Let me tell you, that was a hard gig to pull off in our
sterile environment. I mean, they really had to want
to die. Beyond that, boys were shanking each other
all the time. Eggie Baby drove one into my chest.
It was only much later, when asked about the scar,
that I looked down at it and realized the bastard had
meant to kill me.

God, I hate thinking about all this. I'm gonna stop now and go clear my head. I hope this counts as a good journal entry.

## Chapter 25

"In our short time together, I think not only have you learned to process information, you have also learned how to manage your own words and gestures," Dr. Hayes pointed out.

"I brought some of that with me to the party," I said. "Mama started us on a steady diet of 'be careful of what you say' as a child. She always said that you shouldn't say too much. She says once you put it out there it can't be taken back."

"Your mother sounds like a smart woman. I'd like to know more about her," Dr. Hayes said gently.

"What do you want to know?" I asked flippantly.

"For now I'm just interested in what you would like to tell me."

"I know her birthday, but I'm not sure how old she is. She chain smokes. She's overweight and instead of paying attention to the world around her, mama keeps her nose stuck in cheap romance books."

"You are making it sound like you don't like her very much," the doctor observed.

"Since this whole thing happened everybody makes out like she's some child abusing lunatic. My world was fine as far as I knew. Then cops and all these folks with nicely framed degrees on the wall keep telling me how bad my mother is, how bad my life was. All I ever was, all I know about who I am is gone. I would trade today in a minute for the past with my mom, brother, friends or just my creek. It's all gone. Y'all took it away. Y'all are the villains. How am I supposed to see my mama as a demon?"

"You're blaming the people who helped you. That's not uncommon. Many hostages grow attached to their captors. The brain rationalizes situations, harmonizes information to make life manageable."

"That's about ignorant. She's my mama; she didn't kidnap me!" I said irritably.

"Of course, she's your mother. I'm alluding to the situation in which she kept you."

"I don't get it. You think the way I see my life is all an illusion or make believe so I can get through the night? That's some stupid shit there. I never felt so fucked up until I was taken into custody."

"No, your life has not been a lie. Just your perception of it was and still is distorted," she said. "You are a smart young man. Surely, you understand that the environment she raised you in was both unnatural and unhealthy. That's contributing to your current state of insecurity."

"Insecure. Why hell yes, I'm insecure!" I said and leaped from my seat onto her plump, shiny black sofa. "I had my security stripped away. Before that I didn't know any better. Sure I knew we were different. I didn't panic. I also knew some people had a million dollars and we were different from them, too."

"Our conversation is becoming too abstract. Please sit down. Take a deep breath or two and then tell me what you want me to know about your mother that is not in the police reports or on the news."

"I want you to know about all the good she did." I said as I fell back on to the overstuffed sofa. I bet Dr. Hayes had paid a premium price for the fine piece of furniture, and still it felt as hard as sitting on a cement curb.

"Can you tell me about the good things you recall?"

I thought for a minute. Nothing came to mind. The more I searched my head, the more frustrated I became. I couldn't think of a thing, not a single good deed.

"She had a job. She didn't get paid much, but she worked. Most of the time we didn't have a car, so she had to ride the bus no matter how cold or rainy it was or whatever the situation. She went to work to take care of her family."

"That's certainly a noble trait. Can you see how all adults have a responsibility to work and provide for their households?"

I knew what she meant. I still hadn't been able to think of any good things to mention.

"It's okay. I didn't mean to put you on the spot," Dr. Hayes said, calmly trying to reduce my anxiety.

"No. This one time, I wanted to play baseball. We couldn't afford the registration, so mama got one of the league scholarships for me."

"That was a nice thing to do, but..."

"That's not the point. You see my buddy wanted to play, too. His mom went down to sign him up only to find there were no more scholarships available. So mama sent in his registration with a check. There was no money in the bank, but she figured by the time the check bounced, she would get paid and have the money to cover the registration and the bank fee."

"Interesting," Dr. Hayes mumbled as she scribbled on her pad.

"No, it was the right thing to do. She helped us. She made a difference. You have no right to look down on her or me."

"I don't look down on you. I look at you and I know you are going through something."

We sat for a moment. I wriggled on the uncomfortable sofa.

"Where do you see yourself in this situation? You have pointed out what has been done to you, and given your age, much of it was not your choice, but do you take ownership in anything that has happened?" she asked.

"What do I own in this? Nothing! I was raised in this," I said, my voice rising with each syllable.

Dr. Hayes looked at me in disbelief. I knew she wanted to hear more. I wasn't in the mood to make up a lie. So I continued, "I lugged bag after bag of trash out of the house to the street the night before garbage day. I hid some in the back yard so people wouldn't wonder where all the trash came from. As quickly as I took it out mama threw some cupcake or hamburger wrapper on the floor or some animal came in and marked its territory in a corner. What the hell was I supposed to do about that? What was I supposed to do about that? How do I own that? Huh? Tell me."

She didn't answer. So I told her what I did. "I moved to the basement. That's all I could do. I kept it clean and free of bugs, particularly spiders. That was my fucking ownership."

"I understand this is painful for you and that cursing is a means for you to emphasize your situation, but it's not necessary. I promise you that I know you are hurting and that you've been through something difficult," she assured me.

"Do you know because you attended some important school, or because you sit there behind that pad listening to people who have been crapped on by life? You don't know me. Hell, I don't even know me. You do-gooders even changed my name. And yeah, I'm pointing the finger of blame. I told the Carpenters I didn't want to do it. To make it okay they let me choose the name, and well, I fixed their little red wagons. I picked a new last name, too."

"Where did you come up with the name, Steve Mallory? Is he a celebrity, an athlete or a combination of names from people you know and want to be like?"

"None of the above. I picked Steve because I didn't personally know anybody with that name. So it was like it was new just for me. I came up with Mallory off the top of my head when we were at probate court and I felt like my arm was being twisted into the whole thing."

"Do you understand why the Carpenters wanted you to make the change?"

"Yeah, I get the whole clean break, fresh start, spiritual rebirth business. I wasn't convinced before and for the *record*, I'm still not."

"Do you like being called by your new name?"

"The God's honest truth is I felt more like me when my friends and family called me Fat Boy."

"Did your mother call you that?"

"Jesus, back to my mom again." I realized I had thought out loud. Now I'd have to say more about mama for sure. The young therapist took no punches lying down. She was a force to be reckoned with and somehow I felt like that boded well for my future.

"If you'd prefer we can talk about your father. What was his relationship like with your mother?"

"Nonexistent. They didn't and still don't relate."

"Fair enough, but what is he like?" Dr. Hayes asked while writing on her pad.

"The guy who got my mama pregnant with me didn't have anything to do with the house. So I can't see how I'm *bound* to talk about him."

"Okay. We only have a few more minutes in our session today. Tell me something you'd like me to know about your mother."

I was pissed. Clearly she knew I wanted to move off this topic, but she dragged me back to it again and again. I wanted to scream. Before I realized it, I had done just that it.

"I miss her. I miss my mama."

## Chapter 26

Here's a good journal entry. I met a girl tonight. Her name is Julie. Since I'm supposed to write about my feelings, let me be clear. This girl made me feel good. I want to note that just in case anybody's wondering about the relevance of this entry, I'm very clear on the fact that I have feelings associated with the whole thing. I hope I made that clear enough, especially since I used the words "clear" and "feel" three times each.

I hope it's okay to have fun with these entries. Anyway, here's how it all started. My one and only new friend, Donny, took me to some hippie coffee shop on the north side of town. Lots of kids who wear sandals and drink herbal teas hang out there. I didn't want to go at first, but I went with him because he told me that he met tons of hot chicks at the place. The guys around there showed more interest in chasing after the Grateful Dead than girls. This left us with open season on a fully stocked babe hunt. That sounded like the break I needed from all the heavy thinking and crap I have to do all the time. So, I rolled with Donny.

I saw her from the second Donny and I walked in the door. I hardly noticed anything or anybody else the whole time we ate. My stalker-like staring fell short of subtle. To my absolute shock the angelic object of my fascination came over and introduced herself. I found my thoughts, words and movements all twisted and mangled. Donny made light of the situation and laughed out loud. I didn't care about the unwanted embarrassing attention. I think Julie was flattered by how smitten I acted. Once I gathered my composure we chatted briefly before I invited

Donny to get lost. He was a sport and cut us some slack. After a while Julie and I walked out to the patio and talked until closing time. It turned out Donny worked his magic and met a girl, too. Once the joint closed, the four of us took Donny's car to a small park. It was quiet, secluded and had a pond.

Julie and I took a stroll around the pond. Donny and his new found friend stayed in the car. They got to know each other better in the old fashioned way. Julie and I counted stars in the reflection of the pond. We talked about everything except my mom, brother or my house. This was the first time I felt like I had truly put the old me behind. Of course it had all been perfect until I wrote that line. I don't know if I'll ever see the benefit of doing this journal shit.

I'm mindful that Julie has no idea who I really am. She doesn't even know my real name. So much for honesty, but this process isn't about integrity. Who am I kidding? I don't give a flip. Tonight was magical. I'll keep up this ruse as long as Julie will hang around.

The moonlight illuminated Julie's wispy auburn hair and adorable freckled face. We kicked off our shoes, took off our socks and dangled our feet in the chilly water. Her legs were smooth and creamy white. Chill bumps quickly covered her exposed skin. Julie pressed her small hand in mine. I inventoried her from top to bottom. She looked radiant. I couldn't recall a single thing I had enjoyed nearly as much in years.

Julie pierced the silence and asked, "Do you think of yourself more like Sid Vicious or Johnny Rotten?"

"Who?" I asked. I was equally surprised by the odd question as much as I didn't understand why she broke the precious moment to talk.

"You have heard of the Sex Pistols?"

I shrugged my shoulders. I had no idea what she was talking about, but I didn't want to seem like a dud or a geek.

"Aren't you a Billy Bad ass?" she asked.

"Why would you think that?" I asked.

"You have that jailhouse tattoo." She had noticed the small cross at the base of my wrist. I thought it remained concealed by my watch. Every time Duke came home he had a new tattoo. Since I couldn't be with him, at least I could be like him.

One afternoon after Duke had to go back to the center I went to the creek. I wrapped thread around the end of a sewing needle, dipped it in Indian ink and jabbed it into my skin. What a dumb ass. In retrospect the only people I knew with a homemade tattoo were in the group home or had done time.

I wondered who Julie knew that had been locked up. Had she been behind bars? I didn't ask any questions. I answered. I told her I had been in some horrifying places, but never in jail. She didn't ask when, where or try to compare experiences. All she did was hold my hand. That was nice. I was happy I didn't have to explain the wretched places I had been or the tattoo. Best of all, I didn't have to lie. I would have if it had come to that.

I noticed she had double piercing in her ears and one earring on the top of her right ear. It was my turn to ask a silly question. So I did. I asked if the one on top hurt. She mocked me for not being more creative. Truthfully, I really wanted to know.

Julie sat up. She kissed me softly. She released my hand and pulled the amethyst stone earring out of the top of her ear. "It's a starter," she informed me, just before shoving it into my left ear lobe. I didn't flinch from the slight twinge I felt as she poked me or the sickening sound of my skin giving way as the pointed post torn a hole. Julie licked a speck of my blood from her finger.

"No matter what happens, you'll never forget me. I hope the earring or the pain in your ear will remind you to call me," she said.

Score one for her team. I respond well to pain. A call will come, oh yes ma'am, it will come.

## Chapter 27

I have many times wondered why the Carpenters adopted a non-Jewish child. They knew I had been raised in a very conservative Christian church. They also knew, all too well, about my mama's house and my bad behavior. Still they brought me into their home. The Carpenters take good care of me, but I remain baffled, as I am far from their kind. Why adopt a troubled teenage boy? That takes time, effort and money. Of all of Duke's lessons, I totally accepted the notion that you should take care of your own kind. And, I'm not a Carpenter. As people, Dr. and Mrs. Carpenter work hard to improve their lives and their neighborhood. They are like a sticky-sweet after school special. I can't figure why they brought me in and fouled their own nest.

That's not the point of this journal entry. Tonight I agreed to join them for my first visit to the synagogue. They have always played cool and never made an issue about my going with them. I think that's what made me curious. They're smart people--maybe that was their plan all along. Before we left, Mrs. Carpenter gave me a piece of paper to write any questions I might have from the service. She advised me to keep it discreet as you are not supposed to write during services in the synagogue. I tried to be cool about it, but I had so many questions that I used both sides and had to write on a piece of paper from the pew. I felt kind of embarrassed and ignorant.

She had an answer to all of my questions. Mostly I made a list of differences from what I was used to doing at church. I was shocked they had no Bible reading or lesson. As it turns out, the Rabbi doesn't read Torah on Friday. The Carpenters said they would take me again tomorrow, but I kind of want to back out. I like the Old Testament and all, but I don't think it will make that big of a difference. I feel certain I'm not a good candidate for conversion to Judaism.

As I wrote that last line it sounded harsh to me. I don't mean to be ugly. I think the worship service was beautiful. I loved the prayers even though they were in Hebrew and I didn't understand a word. The cantor made such a pleasing offering that I know God must have rejoiced with the faithful. I offered my own prayers at the end. Surely God got mine mixed in with theirs.

I found the candle lighting ritual peaceful. The thing is that while the ladies were lighting them, I thought about Matthew Chapter 5:16 "…let your light shine before men, so that they may see your good works." I know it was wrong for me to be thinking at that time about something Jesus said, but it's what happened.

When the time came I took a pass on the wine and bread. That seemed a step too far for me and I didn't think it right for a non Jew to take part. I scribbled a question as to how this was different from the body and blood of Jesus. Turns out, the Christian Church borrowed a lot from our Jewish brethren. Pastor Frank never told us that. Maybe he didn't know everything after all. Maybe there's hope for me yet.

## Chapter 28

"I'm in a mood today. Maybe it'll be best if I come back another time," I said, trying to squirm my way out of the weekly trip to the skeleton closet.

"I'd prefer if you stayed. This could be very productive time for you. Let's start with what's bothering you," Dr. Hayes said.

"Of course! I knew it was a gamble."

"It doesn't mean you have lost. You can leave if you want, or you can talk with me and maybe I can help."

"Maybe?"

"You seem to appreciate gambling. Why don't you give it a go? What's on your mind?" Dr. Hayes asked, smiling. Usually she didn't seem so jovial. Perhaps my coming in with an issue in hand perked her up. Her happiness did little to help me. I hoped she had something else in her therapeutic arsenal.

"Julie saw it last night," I said, dismally.

"What did she see? Did she come across a news story about the house you lived in with your mother?"

"No, worse than that. She saw me. She saw the ugliness," I said and rubbed my hand across my forehead and through my hair.

"I want you to take your time. When you're ready I want you to take me step by step through what happened. What it is Julie saw that you think is so awful?"

"I wanted to take Julie to the creek. It's the only thing precious to me." I said. "But I wasn't ready. I wanted to return for the first time by myself. I keep putting it off because I don't know for sure how I'll react. So, I took Julie to a little lake close to my old neighborhood. We took Cokes and snacks. It was almost perfect. We just hung out and dreamed out loud for hours. You'd have been proud of me. We talked and I used the word *feel* about ten or twenty times."

"That certainly sounds like progress. When I first met you, *feel* was a word you rarely used. I am proud of you by the way, especially now. Keep going as you are able." I had grown fond of the gentle yet absolutely forceful way Dr. Hayes kept our conversations moving.

I continued, "It started to rain so we ran for cover under a small pavilion. We stopped talking. We had nowhere to be, so I splashed through the rain to get a blanket. I thought we were going to go from indigo to sunrise.

"I hope you weren't that cheesy with her," said a smiling Dr. Hayes. This giddiness was odd. I'm not sure that it suited her.

"You're cracking me up," I said. "Well, we spread out the blanket. Jules didn't ask why I had one in the car. I was prepared to tell her the Boy Scout thing rather than admit that Dr. Carpenter had required I have it in case I broke down in the wintertime. Anyway, we nestled our heads and looked at the stars. This time we enjoyed them in the heavens, not in reflections of still waters. I moved to kiss her cheek and it happened." I stopped. I didn't see it coming, but my arms and face started tingling. My throat constricted and I could feel tears trying to flee their ducts. I looked away and balled my fists. I blew out a breath and continued. Dr. Hayes didn't flinch at my signs of emotion.

"I saw something," I said, and realized I was gritting my teeth. My face went hot. "I think I need to stop. I'm gonna go for now. I'll try to finish later."

"That's a choice you're welcome to make. Are you sure you can't tell me what you saw?" Dr. Hayes said.

"I wasn't sure what at first," I said without hesitation. "I focused my eyes in the dark. Then it happened. The ceiling moved. I jumped to my feet. The rafters of the pavilion were alive. My body went numb with a lifeless feeling I had known before. It was like Julie had slipped me some hallucinogenic drug."

"Were you using something?" asked Dr. Hayes.

"No! I don't do drugs. I'm fucked up, but I never use drugs," I barked.

"Okay, I'm sorry. What was it that you saw?"

"Spiders. Hundreds of spiders glided across the exposed wooden beams. It was filled with them. There were webs, egg sacks and more spiders than I had ever seen in my life in that infested pavilion." I realized the tears had escaped. My lips quivered. I felt like I was there all over again.

"I take it you are afraid of spiders."

"I'm not afraid of anything. I hate spiders. I kill them," I said with rage boiling in my voice.

"It's okay. It's all over now."

"No. I freaked. I couldn't move. Just like the first time. I fell to the ground and just lay there. Suddenly, I managed make out Julie's voice amid the madness in my head. Then I really freaked. I couldn't believe I let her see me lying there like a baby. I grabbed her by the shoulders and told her to help me. I told her she had to help me. 'It's okay, baby. I'm here,' she said.

"See, Julie didn't want to ridicule you. She was there for you."

"Oh, hell, no she wasn't. There were so many spiders. I needed her to help me. I asked her to help me. I had to kill them. I had to kill them all. She ignored me. She wrapped herself around me and started crying. 'Come on baby, let's get out of here,' she said."

"Seeing you in a face to face situation with the object of intense feelings does not mean Julie saw anything in you that is not understandable," Dr. Hayes said.

"That's still not it. I went with her to the car. I put the blanket in the trunk and then I scrambled back to the pavilion with a road flare and set it on fire. I stood there breathing in the smoke like nectar. I pumped my fists in the air as the flames lit up the night. I reviled in my victory and went into a frenzy of yelling and dancing as the fire decimated the horrid creatures.

I knew the cops or at least the fire department would be along soon. They always ruin everything. So, I finally tore myself away from the beauty of the blaze. By then Julie had crawled into the backseat. She whimpered from her fetal position for me to take her home. I did. The next morning I went back to the lake and celebrated the demise of the spiders some more. Then it hit me. Julie. What had I done?"

"You need to be worried about yourself more than your girlfriend. You are aware that this is the kind of behavior that landed you in treatment, aren't you?" I didn't respond. I had stopped sobbing and was now exuberant, recalling tormenting my tormentors.

"Okay, are you aware that you have confessed to a crime? I'm seeing you on a contract via the court."

"What are you going to do?" I asked soberly. She said nothing for a bit.

"Do you always do that? Do you always kill the spiders like a savage warrior?" she asked.

"Yes, I generally kill them on sight. First, I let the spider know its certain death is at hand and then I bring it about, swiftly and harshly."

"It's interesting that you have never mentioned your fear of spiders to me," Dr. Hayes noted.

"That's because like I told you, I'm not afraid of spiders," I protested. "I kill spiders."

"And *on sight*, as you put it, do spiders always ignite this same rage in you?"

"Yes," I answered without a thought.

"I'd like you to consider that mingled with your rage is anger, fear and pain. The spider has unfortunately come to embody all of that. For you, spiders are the focal point of those emotions that are pent up inside of you. When you encounter them you don't avoid them or remove them. You annihilate them."

"Yeah, I make sure they are dead," I said, not giving much thought to Dr. Hayes' eloquent waxing.

"More than killing spiders, you rid them of shape, form and life forever. Why do you think that is?"

I paused to consider the question.

## Chapter 29

"I had to go back to learn that I didn't have to go back. Does that make sense?"

"Perfect," Dr. Hayes said without looking up from writing hurriedly on her mystery pad.

"Ever since that terrible snowy night when the world autopsied my home life I have felt I'd been dissected while still alive. Even though that left me feeling like most of my nerve endings were exposed, I have wanted to go back. I'm not sure of the motivation. I feel certain it's not about closure. Maybe I needed to know if that's where I belong; to know if I belong anywhere. Perhaps it was a morbid curiosity, or perhaps I wanted to see it all again and discover that it's not as bad as I remember."

"What did you find?" she asked.

"I found our house had been long since leveled. Even though the physical structure had been knocked down, I knew that the memory would linger. Like the missing Library of Alexander the Great, the oral history would long remain after all traces had vanished. I just learned about that," I said proudly.

"It's a good analogy. I'd like to hear more about your visit," she said, redirecting me.

"I suppose the house got plowed pretty soon after the trial against mama. On the way down, I knew it would be gone. It's okay that it is. I guess. I think I wanted to go back to pay homage, to say goodbye. It's just one more thing stripped away. But that's my fault. I waited too long," I said.

"There are occasions in life when it's best to cut the line and throw away the scissors."

"Now that's a good analogy," I said. We both smiled. I knew I needed to keep going. "In the place of our old homestead a three story house stood as if it had been cut from the hillside. The fabulous new place, full of floor to ceiling windows, was built on the slope of what was our backyard. I wondered if the land is a blessing to the family that lives there now, or if it haunts them like it does me. Funny, the whole neighborhood had gone to those much more fortunate.

"Most of the houses and places I knew as a kid were gone. Their memory was erased and replaced with something bigger and better. Only the ground knew the dark story and it kept quiet like a sleeping monster. The lake where my brother loved to fish had been filled in and covered over with Class A office space. The envelope company I fantasized about working in had become trendy loft apartments with artist work space and galleries.

"As I cruised through my old haunts I noticed a house for sale. I went to school with Denise, a girl whose family lived there years ago. Now a new incarnation stood in the place that used to be home to the first girl I ever kissed. I pulled over and took the informational flyer from the real estate agent's box. I nearly choked. The place had been *reduced* to $400,000. I couldn't imagine. I stood on the curb, utterly astonished. Just a few short years ago when I had sat on that very porch and sipped sweet tea, nobody in their right mind would have given four hundred dollars a month in rent for this house, or any other within a five miles.

"I couldn't make sense of the gentrification. I hadn't wanted the neighborhood to slip into something worse than it was, just because I couldn't be there. While at the same time, I had never imagined this would become a vogue place for the upper class. I think I just wanted it to stay just like it was. More and more I have learned that nothing ever stays the same. The revitalization of the cracker box neighborhood hit me as the opposite of the Joni Mitchell classic. The developers planted an oasis over the causeway to Hell.

"I kept riding around hoping that the episode of the Twilight Zone I was living in would soon end. It didn't. The old Stalling place had been remodeled. The top had been popped and the place had new paint, doors and a picket fence. How quaint. I stopped in front and lingered, thinking of all the times I manipulated and maneuvered my way into joining them for dinner. Mrs. Stalling did amazing things with her cast iron skillet."

"As I recall this is the family that first took you to church."

"Yep. The Stallings went to church whenever the doors were open and they did all they could to bring people with them. They are good folks."

"I'm sorry to have interrupted. You are doing great. Please continue," she encouraged.

"When I was sitting in front of their house Mr. Stalling slid out of the front door and plopped into a rocker on the front porch. The chair had been worn and stressed in ways the fancy furniture stores couldn't replicate. I threw the car in park and rushed through the fence toward the spacious porch. Along the way I realized that he may not remember me. My unannounced visit might seem suspicious or even scary. Surely it's unsettling to have a car in front of your house and then a strange guy to come running toward you. I began calling out to ease the shock.

"Mr. Stalling. It's me. It's Fat Boy. Mr. Stalling." He stayed in the chair and smiled as I rapidly moved ever closer.

"Boy, you in need of a new name. Fat Boy seems foolish for a little rail like you," he said, still sitting in his rocker. I took his hand and shook it vigorously.

"Janie, we got company. Come on out here," he bellowed through the screen door.

"Oh, dear, sweet child. Praise God! I'm so happy to see you," Mrs. Stalling said as she ran her hands over my face, caressing it, holding it. "I knew that baby fat would just fall off of you one day." She kissed my forehead.

"We pray for you pret-near every day. I'm so sorry for what happened to you. We wanted to take you and raise you as our own. We told the authorities that we all the time fed you and took you to church pret-near every week. We told them we loved you like our own and that you loved the Lord. We told them we knew you had Jesus in your heart. They didn't pay us no mind. They never answered our calls nor our letters."

"That means a lot to me. Thanks for trying," I said, and hugged her. I remember as a kid she'd ask for a hug by saying, "Come squeeze my neck."

"How are you, son?" Mr. Stalling asked.

"I'm fine. Things are really going okay for me."

"Praise Jesus!" Mrs. Stalling proclaimed. "The Lord blessed you. Jesus blessed you because he knew you have a good heart."

I struggled to comprehend the old hood. Who'd believe a poor kid with no heat or running water ever lived here. It's like my side of town got

up and moved to the right side of the tracks. I could
see the Stallings as the kind to dig in and stay, but
they completely joined the other team with the
expensive and expansive remodeling. Their
renovations were top notch. Mrs. Stalling gave me
the tour and it was as if I'd never been in the house
before.

"You have to stay for dinner. You need a
good meal to put some meat back on those bones of
yours." I knew my recollection of her cooking
wouldn't fail me, but I declined her offer to stay for
dinner. She pleaded with me and offered to make
homemade biscuits, my favorite. She wanted to call
her kids and get them to come over.

I wanted to see them all, and I really wanted
to have the biscuits, but for some reason, I declined.
She compromised and pulled out a plate of cookies
and her photo albums and scrapbooks. I made all
the right cooing sounds about the grandkids. I
managed to say as little as possible when they asked
about my mama and brother. I thanked the Stallings
for their unyielding hospitality and told them I had
an appointment across town. I promised to come
back and see them and go to church. With a litany
of parting remarks I took my leave to see how time
and nature had altered the creek."

"How did that go?" Dr. Hayes asked.

"I didn't go. I chickened out."

## Chapter 30

"Radio silence. Without warning my car and all of its accoutrements went dead. Julie and I had been screaming, more than singing, "Thunder Road" along with the radio. The sudden loss of our back up band caught my immediate attention. The lack of power steering and power brakes had me sit up and take notice for real.

"Julie poked her head out of the window and made pleading hand gestures to get other drivers to make way for us. That, along with her whipping auburn hair and adorable freckled face, caught us some grace. I maneuvered the lifeless car into the emergency lane of the Interstate.

"This car had previously been so fast and responsive to the slightest pressure on the gas pedal that I had named it Response. Giving a car a name is not uncommon; I took it an immature step further. I went to the hardware store and bought lettering for mailboxes and affixed the word *Response* on the back of the car. At this moment she responded to nothing. I turned the key time and time again, to no avail.

"A mystery. I had no idea what had happened to my beloved Response or what to do about it. The not knowing, the powerlessness, the embarrassment burned in me. I tried to walk it off. That wasn't good enough, so when in doubt, I pitched a fit. I yelled at the car until I felt my eardrums quake and my throat constrict. I grew hot, while sweat lined my forehead and filled my palms. Spittle blew out with my every curse. I cursed the car. I cursed my rotten luck. I cursed my life and then I cursed Julie.

Gently and shyly she said, 'It's not far to the next exit. We can walk and call for a tow truck.'

"'I ain't calling no tow truck. God damn this shit!' I screamed and pumped my foot like I was kicking something. 'Everything was going just fine. Why the fuck did this have to happen? I'll leave this piece of junk on the road before I pay for a tow truck!'"

"'If you don't have the money we can get it towed to my house. I'm sure my parents will pay and you can make it up to them later,' Julie said softly.

"Oh hell no! I said I ain't getting a tow. I didn't say shit about money." I ran up to her side of the car and howled, "Don't you ever!" I stopped and snatched her out of the seat and off the ground. "Don't ever make out like I can't afford something. I'd just as soon kill you for less!"

I dropped her and she plummeted to the street. On the way down Julie raked her back against the side mirror. It jabbed her and made a terrible shriek as it broke. She hit the roadway with a yelp and a sob. The mirror dangled like a yo-yo.

"'Oh my god. Look what you have done,' I cried out. 'You little bitch. You broke my damn mirror. Shit. A mirror of all things. Like I need more bad luck.'

Julie's tear soaked eyes surveyed the mirror and then they focused on me. I looked at her and through her. I burned with rage.

"'Oh, you are going to pay for that. You're gonna get it fixed. I don't have time for this shit. Look what you did!' I pointed at the swaying mirror as if it were new to Julie. Cars zipped by as we acted out our horror story on the road side. She gulped down her pain, tears and words. I didn't.

"I went off. I screamed so loudly that my scratchy voice sounded like a territorial banshee. I tried to keep spewing my venom, but my voice, like the car, failed me. Only tidbits came out audibly as I raged.

"I had more to say. Julie cried. Neither suited my mood. Finally, my frustration boiled over. I kicked the fender well of the car only an inch to the left of Julie's head. The metal buckled inward. My action and the car's reaction played in slow motion for me. I saw the damage being done. It registered. I knew I couldn't unring this bell. I gnashed my teeth. I looked at the dent in the car and began cursing incoherently. Then I looked down at Julie. I think maybe I should have killed her."

"Now, calm down a bit. You should have killed her over a mirror? That's a little harsh, wouldn't you agree?" asked Dr. Hayes. She hadn't said a word for nearly thirty minutes. She had just let me unload.

"That whole night was harsh. I said it and I meant it. I don't know what, but something died in both of us that night. Whatever it was made life into something it's not supposed to be."

"Can you identify what you lost now that you have re-lived it?"

"Are you serious? If it ever makes sense to me I'll do all I can to resurrect what was lost," I said. "Without it I don't know if I'll ever be the same."

"Then we are going to have to do some detective work. Let's start with the car. Tell me about it," said Dr. Hayes.

"Are you serious? After what I just said, you want me to tell you about a damn car?"

"The situation you just described was highly emotionally charged. It had as much to do with the problems of the car as it did with you or Julie. Do you want to get to the base of the matter or not?" she asked.

"What a deal. I'd much rather talk about Response than my feelings. Here you go. She's a classic Chevy. I use the term classic, as she was twenty years old when Dr. Carpenter first bought her. I know getting this car ran against a lot of the stuff he believes. Normally, he would never have purchased an old gas guzzling, emissions spewing American car. Funny the things one does for love. Response has gray primer and a brown bonding agent on the front end to accent to her original pale blue. The canvass covering of the roof is peeling. She's a five hundred dollar car housing an eight hundred dollar radio and nearly two thousand dollars worth of tires and rims. My baby has to roll in style."

"Yes indeed, you are emotionally attached to the car, but if you care so much about the car, why haven't you had it painted?"

"I did all the body work. I never managed to find the time to take it to a paint shop." I paused and then said, "Honestly, I hate the idea of paying for it and it's not something I can do myself."

"Thanks for your honesty. I know you are working hard at this. Unfortunately, you finished the easy part. Now I need you to think about the object of your anger. Was it Response, Julie or were you angry with yourself?'

"I didn't do anything. I was just driving down the road minding my own business. And Julie was the one with the stupid shit about me not having any money."

"Let's put our detective gumshoes back on for a minute. I want you to think about this one part at a time. How did it make you feel when the car broke down?"

"You don't need a detective to know that the car made me look stupid. It embarrassed me and I couldn't be the champion and fix it. I'm no mechanic. I can change a tire and that's about all."

"Great work," she said. "You said it yourself. You got angry not at the car, but what the car did as an extension of you. It made you look stupid, embarrassed you, and it made you feel powerless and inadequate."

"Hooray. 'Great work,' my ass," I said, showing my annoyance. "An old car beat me down like a squealing little punk. Now, how on earth is that supposed to help me?"

"You identified the source of your anger. That's how it helps. Now, I need you to tell me about the rage that followed. The car did something you didn't understand. It hurt you, its caregiver. You disliked that. The car abandoned you." The young therapist took no punches lying down. She was a force to be reckoned with and I continued to think that boded well for my future.

I had nothing to lose, so I answered. "The rage is hard to explain. In terms of controlling it, I liken the experience to vomiting." Dr. Hayes gave no indication as to her appreciation of the metaphor.

"The way I see it is I can feel it when either one is coming on. It's like it has its own announcer. Ladies and gentlemen, get ready, here come the crazies. I bounce all over the place filled with adrenaline and I feel like I can do anything in the world. Even once it starts and my mind is racing, I know what I need to do as protective measures.

The thing is, I have to make a decision whether or not to stop it. Once it starts, both puking and fury are vile and I understand something toxic is in my mind and body that needs to escape. I let go and ride it out, hoping to be purified. In hindsight, I detest being sick and being so angry, but when it's over sometimes I do feel a little bit better.

"And what happens those other times?" she asked without hesitation.

"I get worse."

Dr. Hayes placed her pad between her leg and the arm of her chair. She held her sharpened pencil up close to her glasses. She lowered it and tapped the point twice before placing it on a stylish side table. "You are describing the classic symptoms of someone who is bipolar, save the bouts with euphoric mania."

"You have never talked about what's wrong with me. Is this a breakthrough? Does this mean you can help me do something about the madness that is my life?" I asked, perking up from retelling my haunting tale.

"I'm sure you don't feel it, but you have a breakthrough in most of our meetings. As hard as you work against me occasionally, you are making good progress toward trusting and listening to others and yourself. All of your work is helping you. We may be able to reduce the harshness of your outbreaks. In the past, we have been very successful treating bipolar patients with treatment and medication."

"Look here, I don't know much about this bipolar thing. When I was coming up they talked about people being schizophrenic. As I understand, that means something like a person has two identities."

"You are close in a crude way, but it's much more complex and schizophrenia and bipolar are different animals altogether."

"Animals. Nice word choice. Anyway, I thought of schizophrenia because to me bipolar by definition means two different things. Here's the deal. My whole life I have been raised as two different people. There was one that went in the house and the other one outside of the house. They live on two different poles. Since the house, I'm this new guy with a new name on the outside and the same old redneck on the inside. The way I look at it, all of my personalities come more from nurture than nature. I was taught how to act and all that I know. Pills can't help me with that."

"Yes, you did train your brain how to think and how to act and what acceptable payouts were. Medical therapy can help rewire those patterns in your brain." Dr. Hayes said.

"You don't get it. First, my brother trained me by actions and dread. That's deep in me now. Drugs can't change that. Second, he's an addict and he knows it. To keep me from being one he used fear and pain. That's the message I relate to and so drugs aren't an option."

"Listen to yourself. You are addicted to the chemicals that release in your brain when you are angry.

"I'm not addicted to shit!" I stated.

"Hear it how you will. Your wiring has to change," she said emphatically.

"Or what?"

"Next time you might hurt Julie instead of the car."

"I already did and I haven't laid a hand on her," I admitted.

"You've got to trust me.  You have got to change your ways."

"If I did, you can't guarantee that the guy with the new wiring won't have anger or that I'll like him any better.  I have to learn to control the beast.  I'm afraid to kill it."

## Chapter 31

"I have to tell you I'm more than a little surprised that Julie continues to show an interest in continuing to have any association with you, much less being your girlfriend," Dr. Hayes said forthrightly.

"What's that supposed to mean?" I asked and sat upright from my restful slouch on the sofa.

"Don't be offended," she said. "From my position it's somewhat surprising to say the least. Look at the situation from my vantage point. Just from the things I know, and I'd venture to guess that you haven't told me everything, this young woman must see you as boorish."

"I thought your job was to help me rebuild or build esteem and confidence, not to tear down my playhouse," I said, defensively.

"Professionally, I'm bound to be brutally honest with you for your own good," Dr. Hayes said. "Don't hear me as being hurtful. Look at what you have told me. I know she witnessed the event when you tried to burn down a structure just to kill a few spiders."

"There were hundreds of them," I corrected.

Dr. Hayes ignored my statement and moved to the next example. "Surely, you know that you grossly overreacted on the occasion when your car broke down."

"It wasn't the car. She made out like I couldn't afford paying to have it towed," I said as if my explanation mattered.

"You know that's not the point. You displayed physical aggression toward her."

I cringed, reliving the moments Dr. Hayes had mentioned and others she hadn't. As far as I thought I had come, I still acted like an animal and seemingly had no control over myself. I went into self-protective mode and burrowed into the corner of the sofa with my arms tight around my midsection.

"Maybe she loves me," I suggested boldly.

"That's possible. I suppose. It's really not my intent to demean your relationship with Julie. It's been my experience that most young women who are not bound by marriage, children or finances don't take very long to exit relationships prone to violence."

"I don't like what you are saying," I said.

"Do you deny any of the events with Julie you have told me about?" Dr. Hayes asked.

"No."

"Do you deny that they were violent?" she asked so rapidly I felt like she was reading from a script.

"No, but you make it sound like I'm not worth a little forgiveness."

"Would you stay with her or forgive her if your roles were reversed?"

I considered the possibility and Dr. Hayes posed another question. "What if someone treated your mother that way?"

## Chapter 32

This whole thing seems retarded to me. I mean, who writes a letter and doesn't send it? How dumb is that? The best I can figure, it doesn't matter what I think. Dr. Hayes is hell bent on having me write this stupid letter. In case I do give this to you, mama, you should know that Dr. Andrea Hayes is the psychologist I have to go to see all the time. It's a drag. She's nice enough and good looking and all, but she makes me do all this talking and processing. It gets on my nerves.

I know good and well that I'm not supposed to write this letter to tell you about her, the Carpenters or any of that stuff. I'm supposed to tell you how I feel now and what living in the house was like for me. Jesus, I don't know how to start. I guess I'm supposed to make this a real letter. Dr. Hayes says it will be best if I'm blunt. I hope you understand. It's supposed to be for my own good. So, here goes.

Dear Mama:

I reckon I'll pass on the traditional greetings and get right to the point of this letter. There were things I hated about life early on. I mean, before they took us away from each other. I hated being fat, I hated not knowing about my father and I hated you wouldn't let Duke live with us all the time. People smarter than me keep saying those things were all beyond my control. Maybe some of it was even beyond your means of control.

I can't make any excuses for the fact that most of all I hated that fucking house. At the time, I didn't realize how the place affected me. As I look back it was that gross ass house that caused my

headaches and stomach pains. I worried constantly
that we would be discovered. I knew it was wrong.
I despised 1857 Belle Meade Street, NW. I can't
believe you allowed us to live there. For many
years I pretended to be thankful that we had a house
at all. But, that rat hole was a pit and it did
something to me I can't explain. I was and still am
ashamed of how we lived. Back then I lived in
constant fear that someone would find out. Now
that they have I live in worse fear that people will
recognize me.

When I was eight, Frankie Powell pushed
through the taped cardboard of a broken window in
the kitchen. He saw inside the house. I caught him
and freaked out. I didn't know what to do. He was
laughing at me. He kept laughing and laughing. He
pointed his finger and rolled out in the yard,
laughing hysterically. I picked up a stick from the
yard and beat him until my arm got tired of
swinging the stick. I remember you asked why we
were not friends anymore. It was because his
mother wouldn't let him talk to me anymore. I'm
not sure if it was because I hurt her son so badly or
if he told her what he saw. I lived all of my life in
fear of him because I knew he had seen my dark
and terrible secret. I often plotted to kill him.

That kind of rage increased over the years. I
terrorized kids, adults, animals and anybody that
would let me have a round with them emotionally
or physically. I'll never be able to apologize to the
many people who were the victims of the hateful
and malicious things I said and did to them. I was
hurting and I wanted to hurt others. I did hurt
myself and others, and that hurt was even worse
when I'd lie in the bed at the end of the day. I'd
think about what I had done.

I have been dancing around this, but I have to say it's your fault. You did this to all of us. You did this to your sons. Even though you never raised a hand to hit us, you beat the life out of Duke and me. What we did with our fists, you did with that house. We were just kids, your kids. I didn't do anything to you and you sent my brother away and left me to live with garbage, roaches, rats, possums and spiders. I am so afraid of spiders. I hate them. We had no heat, we had no water, we didn't have a refrigerator, we had no stove or oven. Sometimes you let the power get turned off. How could you let this happen? I was just a boy.

And all of that impacted colon stuff. That was a farce. I can't believe you troubled to FINALLY take me to a doctor. You were much too smart not to know that I didn't use the bathroom because there was a gaping hole in the fucking floor. The bathroom had NEVER been cleaned even before the pipes froze. I had "accidents" because I just didn't want to use the bathroom. Eventually, it had to come out.

So here I am an angry young man. I pee in the yard. I still wait to the last possible minute to go to the bathroom. I obliterate spiders on sight. I seek out the heat, because I loathe the cold. It was easy to stay cool in that house, hell I never worried about a fan or anything. But it was cold in the winter, damn cold, especially once I moved into the basement. And that is another thing. I was not even a teenager and you let me move into a cement and dirt room with no windows and NO DOOR. There was no heat and no water even before the pipes froze. My God, woman, what were you thinking?

Now, I'm older and I'm beginning to understand the rigors of adulthood and the flow of finances. But, I didn't choose to give birth to and raise children. There should be consequences for the way I suffered. I yelled at you when that's all I could do. I know I could have arranged to see you when you were in jail and in the halfway house. I didn't. It wasn't that I wasn't ready. I hoped my not coming hurt you. I did the same to Duke. I treated him badly as I only see him as part of that thing that caused me such pain. Besides, he was older. He knew. The way I see it, he got out one way or another. He should have come back for me. No, I had to live there the longest. Well, fuck both of y'all.

As part of my "treatment," I am supposed to forgive you, but I have just now gotten around to recognizing that my frustration, my hate and fear come from that hell hole and from you. I could have kept it all buried forever. No, I had to talk, talk, talk. Get it out. Process it. Let it go. Bullshit! Now, I have unearthed it and I can't even get an aspirin for the hurting it brought along for the ride.

It's no wonder why I treat girls so badly. I have been such a dick because I had to be a hard ass, or so I thought. I cannot live the rest of my life and remain emotionally unavailable. I cannot become the inconsiderate and uncaring thing that I deplore. I learned not to talk about anything as a kid. I could not talk about Duke, my dad, school, the house, Duke's father, my health problems. As time went on, I screwed up my own life and created my own secrets. I cut school, stole, fought and other stupid shit.

I've done all this crap with the Boy Scouts in the community seeking redemption and acceptance, but all I got was a handful of cheeky badges. I haven't been to church since I moved in with the Carpenters. They've been good to me, but I plan to blow their place as soon as I am of age. I have no attachment to you anymore. I have no family. I don't even know how to be honest with people. I avoid intimacy. I detest eating with people. I don't feel like a son to the Carpenters. I'm just a tenant in their house.

I'm afraid of talking about myself or my home life, even with the Carpenters. The littlest thing sets me off and I yell and scream. Once I calm down then I eat too much to self-medicate to make it better. Now, I'm obsessive about exercise and other unimportant foolishness.

I wonder if Duke really had mental issues or if he was smart enough just to get out of the house. For all his street smarts he always went on about how much he loved you. I think that was what he thought he was supposed to say to me. Maybe Duke acted like a mental case to keep away from you. I know for a fact when I acted like a maniac in school I was trying to be with him not because he was my big brother, but because he had a warm clean place to live.

I still worry somehow that those horrible things will come back. I have nightmares about being back there in that hellish dimension. I can't even be comfortable in the Carpenters' house. I panic when someone comes to the door. I fear somehow, someway it's not right and that I'm not supposed to have a nice and clean house, a normal life. I have stomachaches, real physical pain, when people come inside the house. This has caused me too much stress over the years. It ends now.

Mama, what you did was fucked up. It was stupid and irresponsible. I fail to see how I can ever move past this. I am very angry right now. I don't get how writing this letter is helpful. I don't feel better. I'm furious.

I don't want to be like you or Duke. I have choices to make. I have to make it different. I'm already messed up. I can't interact with others like a normal person. I try to resolve everything with violence. I must do all I can to move past the hurt, pain and frustration that I have known and my miserable life experiences with regard to family, home and emotional life together. I want to call you more mean names. But it isn't coming out as I had hoped. But hear this; I will not be like you. I will not be like Duke. You made bad choices. You caused me to suffer for far too long.

Today, I admit to my pain. Today I admit that I could not control it. Today, I begin to work harder to be better than where I came from and to be the person I want to be. Today, I begin to appreciate that who and where I am in life today is not a sham. No one is out to get me. I'm not out to get anybody. I'm not in any trouble and I did nothing to create 1857 Bellemeade Street. I did live there once. Honestly, I knew it was wrong. I did choose to remain silent about our horrific situation. Those were my choices and I accept my responsibility. I also choose to get on with my life. So on I go.

If I'm supposed to feel better, I don't. All writing this letter did was make me mad. I want to kick the shit out of somebody. I'm done with this and I'm done with you. The truth is the most

disturbing thing after all this is that I'm as touched
as Duke.  I love you and I'd forget about everything
if you'd just come and get me.  Good bye, good
luck and I sincerely pray God will have mercy on
you.

Your son.

# Gathering
## Chapter 33

"I found Julie's breaking point and pushed her beyond it," I said smugly.

"What did you garner from that endeavor?" Dr. Hayes returned my smugness.

"An ex-girlfriend it would seem, but you predicted as much."

"Steve, I have no idea what has happened. Why don't you take a moment and tell me about it."

"Doesn't matter, she's gone," I said.

"Yes, it matters," Dr. Hayes said. "I want to help you. I was trying to suggest that you control your anger with her and you misread my words. We don't have to talk about it now or ever for that matter."

"It's a mess. I might as well get it out there," I said, while rubbing my forehead. "Julie and I were on our way to get dinner. I was taking her to a nice place. Once we got there I planned to spring a big surprise I had for her. The night before, I had camped out at a music store to get concert tickets for Bruce Springsteen.

"I got there early enough to land a primo place in line. I only needed two tickets and with a six ticket limit I hustled the other four slots. I made enough money to cover our two seats and to pay for a fine dinner out. To top it off I had a blast spending the night on the sidewalk of Ponce de Leon Avenue. Wow, what a night. I met a woman who claimed to be Geraldine Ferraro and a one armed man who said he was Jesus. He smelled of urine and cursed us all to Hell, as none of the urban campers would give him a cigarette."

My pause didn't draw the response I intended.

"Making light of others isn't helpful and I'd prefer if you held such comments to yourself, unless they lend to the story"

"Okay, I'll get to it. I picked up Julie and tried to hide my anticipation. I hadn't decided exactly how to share the good news with her. She was going to be thrilled. We pulled up to a gas station, one where they have a guy out in a little glass box to take your money so you don't have to go all the way in the store to pay for your fuel.

"The boy in the box smiled and gave a shy and somewhat covert wave to Julie. She looked away, but not at me. I could tell she was trying to go invisible. I used to try that back in grade school when I knew the odor in the room from not bathing was coming from me. As I pumped the gas, I noticed the guy in the glassed-in box struggled not to make eye contact with me, even when I paid. I glanced in the car and Julie continually tried in vain to go undetected. I didn't need an upbringing in lies or the tutelage in nonverbal gestures from the Carpenters to know there was something afoot here.

"My intent was to draw whatever it was out of Julie causally, but that night I discovered I had wide green stripe of jealousy painted right on me. Most of the time when I got upset I was either in a fight or I had no earthly idea what was wrong with me. The feeling that had come over me just considering that Julie may like this guy or had cheated on me sent me to a new place on the hostility spectrum. I drove erratically. At a stop sign I snapped a look at Julie and our eyes admitted we knew. We both knew what we wished we didn't. I pulled the car behind an abandoned pump house that belonged to the water authority.

"What did you do?" I bellowed. My words echoed in the darkness of the night.

"Nothing," she murmured.

"Don't tell me 'nothing'!" I said, "I saw y'all then and I can see you, now. You can't hide shit. Now tell me, what did you do?"

"Take me home," Julie demanded.

"Happily, after you tell me what I need to know."

"Nothing. We didn't do anything," she said.

"We? Huh? So you do know him."

Julie turned and pressed herself to the passenger door. In a low voice she said, "The night the car broke down. I didn't want to go home. I didn't want to be alone. I went to Maleah's house. He was there with her boyfriend. We hung out. That's it."

"That ain't shit. That's not the half of it. What did you do?" I repeated.

"Stop it!" she screamed. "You know what we did. I was hurting. I was afraid. I was afraid of you. He let me forget that horrible night. I wish I could forget the whole awful thing."

"You don't know fear or hurting. You can believe this, after tonight neither of you will ever forget what it's like to be afraid or to feel pain. Ever!" I cranked the car and spun the wheels, kicking up dirt and gravel for an inordinate amount of time. My first thought was to go straight back to the gas station. I decided Julie would only get in the way and if she even thought about protecting the slime ball, and then I didn't know what I'd do. I took her home.

The car skidded to a stop in front of her house. Julie didn't move. So, I leaned across her and opened the passenger door. I paused for a millisecond. The smell of her hairspray always reminded me of our first night at the pond. She used the same stuff every day. To smell it meant to be with Julie. I breathed it in. Tonight was to be the last night with her. I had never been more certain in my life. I had driven away my first love, Rhonda. I guess I'm just not suited to be the relationship kind of guy. My time with Julie had expired.

Then time stopped. While trying to calm me down Julie called me by my real name. She said she knew everything about me. She said she knew what I aimed to do and begged me to let it go. She said I had changed. Let it go, she repeated. She would help me. I didn't know what to think. I didn't think at all. Crack. I cracked. The windshield cracked when I punched it.

I wanted something else to hit, something to hurt. I fixed my eyes on the shattered windshield. I could barely see the road. Ironically, the shatter pattern looked like an icy spider web had been placed over the car. It had just been a month or so since I fixed the passenger side mirror, but now because of Julie, my car had been damaged, again.

"Get out!" I howled. Julie didn't flinch. I grabbed her by the wrists and pulled her out through my door and dropped her on the curb. I yanked the car in reverse and slammed on the brakes. The motion brought Julie's door to a deafening close. Then I popped the car in gear and squealed the tires as I raced to wreak havoc on her little boyfriend.

I barely made it through the intersection before I noticed the blue strobe lights. I got pulled

over by the police. He stopped me because of the
windshield. My license, registration and insurance
were all in order. Still, the officer instructed me to
step out of the car. He asked how much I had to
drink in the course of the evening. I explained I had
never had a drop of alcohol in my life. He
proceeded to give me several field sobriety tests. I
passed them all.

"Boy, I been at this a while. You aren't
drunk, but something's tearing at you and it's not
clear to me what it is." he said.

"I'm fine, officer. Can I go now?" I asked.

"No, not yet. Have you had a fight with
your little Miss Missy tonight?"

"That's not illegal if I had. And it's none of
your business." I said, realizing that I probably
wasn't helping my cause by being an ass.

"Look boy, being behind the wheel while
you are overly emotional is as bad as driving under
the influence of drugs or alcohol," the cop said.

"We just broke up," I admitted, hoping to
get him off my back.

"Just like that for no reason?"

"No. I found out she's been with another
guy. So I punched the windshield," I said,
surveying my knuckles. For the first time I noticed
I had been bleeding.

"Better you hit the car than the other guy.
Buying a new windshield is a sight cheaper than
going to jail, getting bailed out, getting a lawyer,
going to court, paying fines and fees. It's a big
hubbub mess, I tell you. You're lucky just to have
skinned up a fist."

"I don't feel lucky."

"Believe me, you are. You're lucky I'm in a
good mood. Look here, you live pretty far out of

my jurisdiction.  Tell you what, I'll follow you as far as I can and then I want you to drive carefully and straight to your house and get this car off the road.  You got it?

"Yes, sir.  I've got it," I said.

"Good.  When you get home, take a long, cold shower.  Wash it off and let it go.  You're young and believe me there will be more girls.  Good looking boy like you.  There'll me a lot more.  Come on, let's go," the policeman said.

At first I had every intention of taking a different route back to the gas station once the cop split.  I planned to go all group home on that little fucking skeezer.  The more I drove with the police officer in my rearview mirror the clearer it became.  I thought about how I had pushed Julie away.  It was me.  I pushed her to him.  It was my fault.  I was to blame as much as anybody.  I couldn't punch that reality out of anybody.  I might as well hit a brick wall, and I had done enough of that in my short life.  Worse than anything, somehow Julie knew who I was.  I had no idea how that had happened.  I couldn't figure how she found out, but she had.  I decided to do what mama would do, avoid it, avoid it all.  By now Julie had surely warned the boy in the box.  I calmed, not much, just enough to go home."

Dr. Hayes said nothing.  She didn't even busy herself with the dangerously sharp pencil and pad.  She had a look much like I must have had when I first realized I busted my windshield.  I wriggled on her uncomfortable couch and feared this amounted to the calm before the storm.

"Hey, do you like Springsteen?  If you do, I've got two tickets I can let you have at a fantastic price." My puerile attempt to lighten the mood got lost in the vast silence.

"You continue to make excellent progress. You took ownership in the situation. You considered consequences and you calmed down. I don't think you would have done any of that a year ago. You made a good choice. You can be proud and respect yourself for that," Dr. Hayes said. I didn't see that coming and didn't hear the compliment.

"A year ago I'd have killed that dude. I'm not sure if time makes a difference because my brother would punish me if he knew how I laid down. He'd lose respect for me if he ever knew."

"Your brother is self-destructive."

"And I'm not?" I quipped.

"You engage in self-sabotaging behavior, but you don't want it to end," she said.

"Yeah. I can see that. I mess things up, and I probably always will as long as I'm under the fang." I paused. "In your professional opinion, do you think I'll ever be well?"

"That's up to you," Dr. Hayes said. "If you keep working and making rational choices, I think you can live a happy and balanced life."

"As a happy and balanced boy, will I always get dumped on?" I asked.

"Life is full of unpredictable situations, some of which we find uncomfortable or distasteful. That's part of the work we have to do. You must come to understand that your actions have consequences and that when unforeseen problems pop up, you should deal with them in rational ways.

"Rational," I repeated. "When a guy has sex with my girlfriend, I think it's completely rational to want to have a slugfest."

"In the human psyche, that is a standard response; however, rationale comes in when you separate actions from fantasy," Dr. Hayes said in a tone that was compassionate and empathic.

"I'm not fantasizing. I'm a fighter. I'll fight and I'll go with anybody," I said, scooting to the edge of the sofa.

"I've read your reports. I know what you are capable of doing. Surely you know it's a fantasy to think you can win every fight."

"I haven't won all of my fights," I admitted.

"Then why do you insist on engaging in violence as a means of resolution?" she asked.

Still perched on the edge of the sofa, I answered, "When I come for a fight, I don't focus on the winning, when there is nothing else to do but fight, my intention is to inflict pain such that my adversary doesn't forget what happened and why."

"How does that serve you?"

"The other guy remembers," I said.

"What is it that you hope he will remember after the fight?" Dr. Hayes asked.

"He will remember what happened. He will remember who he tied it up with and why. He'll remember me."

"Steve, for all the progress you have made, that's the most self-absorbed thing I've ever heard you say."

"You may want to re-read your reports. Shoot, by now you should know I don't hit girls. Julie pierced my ear, so I'll never forget her. In return, I needed to tattoo myself into her memory one way or another. It's the same as giving a guy a beating; it lets me leave my mark on him. Don't be misled, it's not all about me. When it's all done we're fused in some lingering way."

## Chapter 34

"You look good," Mama said. Her voice startled me. At first I thought she was asleep. I had been standing in her hospital room for several minutes. Mama's voice rang as true as anything I had ever known, yet I hardly recognized her. Her face was puffy and her skin had a yellow tint. She looked terrible. With all the tubes and medical gadgetry attached to her, I had wondered if she was in coma, medically induced or otherwise.

"How'd you lose the weight?" she asked.

My staring had given away my shock. I tried to cover it up. "I've taken to jogging when I'm irritated," I said. "I end up running a lot. I'm always running. It keeps me out of trouble and as an added little bonus I've lost a couple of pounds," I said. Dr. Hayes had convinced me to go and see my mother as part of my healing. Finding her like this in the hospital I felt just about everything imaginable, but healing was not a part of the mix. I knew my speech and disposition lacked confidence. I figured I'd try to stand still and not say too much. I was good at the latter.

"The new trim look suits you. I like it. All the young ladies must be chasing you around these days."

"Yeah, girls pay me some attention now and then. It's not just about the weight. Girls liked me before I thinned out," I said.

"I know they did. I wasn't trying to hurt your feelings. You look good, son. Enjoy it. That's all I'm saying," she retorted.

I didn't say anything. I stood staring at her.

"Is there a special little lady in your life?" she asked.

"Uhh, well, I don't want to talk about it."

"I'm so glad we are having this time together. You don't have to be so stiff. I'm still your mother. Tell me about your girl," Mama said.

"Julie. Her name is Julie. We're not together anymore, I don't think. I really don't want to talk about her."

"Okay, well are you going to come over here and give me a hug and some sugar or are you just going to stand there?"

"I think I'll just hang for a minute," I said.

"You were never the warm and fuzzy type. At least come sit down and tell me why it is that you came here. Why now?" Mama asked.

"It appears neither of us are much for the touchy feely stuff," I said. "What's wrong with you? Why are you in here?" I asked, while remaining standing.

"You should never answer a question with a question," Mama said.

"You're not going to tell me what's wrong with you, are you?" I asked and moved closer to her bed.

"It's nothing. Don't worry. I'm going to outlive the cockroaches."

"Interesting metaphor," I said. Mama used to tell me there was no use trying to rid our old house of roaches. She said they're durable and have grown immune to poisons. She said they were here with the dinosaurs and would always be around. The recollection caused me to smile involuntarily.

I took another step closer to her and said, "You know I can go out and talk to a nurse or find your doctor. So, are you going to tell me what's the matter with you or do I have to find out for myself?"

"How did you know I was in the hospital?" Mama asked.

"Okay, you're not going to tell me. I'm glad to see some things haven't changed." I said.

"Are you going to answer my question or are we going to just keep jousting?" Mama asked.

"I'm not without resources," I said pompously. "I always knew where you were. I went to your halfway house and met a pleasant woman smoking in the stairwell."

"Jane Boyd," she said, in a knowing voice. "Curse her. How did you ply the information out of her?"

"I'm telling you, I'm a man of means. Don't be too fast to curse your friend. She only told me about the hospital, but she was loyal to you and didn't tell me how long you had been here or why. You were always good at getting people to go along with you and protecting your secrets." I said

"All right, now I know how you found me. I still don't know why."

"I came here to deal with the past. That's what my head doctor says I need to do," I declared.

"How are you supposed to do that?" Mama asked.

"I don't know. I hoped it'd come to me once I got here."

"Okay, so you are here. Tell me what's been going on with you. Where are you living?"

"I was adopted."

"I know that. I had to sign the papers," she said, dejectedly.

"The Carpenter's house is south of the city."

"Is a good neighborhood? Good schools and all that?" she asked expectantly.

"No, it's a crappy in town area that is slowly being bought up by white liberals and homos."

"Be nice. You've lived in a rough part of town before. Have you made new friends other than, what was her name? Julie?"

"Yes, and yes. But I don't want to talk about them."

Mama painstakingly readjusted herself on the bed. I suggested that she pull up the sheet, as hospital gowns are far too revealing. She sighed at me and tried to cover up. All the tubes in her arm and clips on her fingertips made the simple task nearly impossible. I had to reach over and help her. She placed the palm of her hand on my forearm. I flinched and cautiously pulled my arm back, largely because a mother's touch never changes. The purpose of my visit wasn't a happy reunion. That could come later, if possible.

"I know there's something you're not saying. What is it? Is something wrong with your brother? Do you need money?" Mama asked.

"No. As far as I know Duke continues to enjoy room and board compliments of the state or county or whoever pays the bills. I'm here to talk. That's it."

"Talk? That's new!" she said laughingly.

"Comedy isn't your strong suit. Let it go. I'm here because…Well, Dr. Carpenter, that's my adopted dad. He's a psychotherapist and Dr. Hayes, she's my shrink, and they both wanted me to write a letter to you. It's not one I'm supposed to send. They think it was supposed to be…cathartic, yeah, I think that's the word."

"You've learned a lot of good words. Write the letter. It'll probably do you good just like they said. You can even give it to me if you want. I

don't think I'll be surprised at anything you have to
say."

"I already wrote it. At first I felt kind of
stupid writing a letter I had no intention of mailing.
I only did it to get them off my back. Once I began
writing it, I stopped because I felt stupid and got
sort of mad. I kept on writing to save myself lip
service about not doing it. The more I wrote, the
madder I got. By the end I was frothing at the
mouth."

"Are you going to give the letter to me, read
it to me or what?" Mama asked.

"No. I already told you that's not the point
of writing the letter," I said.

"Okay, then. I'm glad you wrote a letter to
me that you don't plan to give me, but I still sense
you came all this way for more than to tell me that."

"Wow, I don't remember you being so
matter of fact before."

"You're not the only one in therapy. It's
part of my treatment to say what's on my mind and
to be direct," she said straightforwardly. I didn't
know this side of her. If her frankness was part of
her new personality, I didn't think I would like it
too much. In fact, I already didn't like it, not at all.
Of course I didn't say that to her. Being completely
forthcoming was not in my treatment plan, not yet.

"For me all they want is to talk, talk, talk.
That's all I've been asked to do in the past couple of
years," I complained.

"Do it," Mama admonished. "It might help
you. Getting things off your chest can make a big
difference." This was the second time she urged me
to comply with things the woman I knew would
never have condoned in a million years.

"I know you didn't just say that. You, Grandmamma, Granddaddy and Duke always said 'hold your tongue.' Now you say talking is good for me. What's all that about?"

"Son, our way wasn't necessarily the best way. We couldn't have talked before, but now that everything's out in the open, it may well just be the right medicine for you, for all of us," Mama said.

"Everything is not out in the open. If you think talking is so grand, then why don't you tell me why you never tried to contact me? I know your court sentence didn't keep you from talking to me on the phone or in person." I said, raising my voice.

"Son, it's more complicated than that," she said.

"They took me away and I knew that wherever Duke was, after what happened they'd be sure not to let him escape ever again. The police took you away like a common criminal," I said. Mama didn't respond fast enough so I kept going. "It's funny, after a while I figured that you probably felt liberated by the whole thing. You got an opportunity to move on with your life and you took it, leaving us behind as casualties."

"Son, I wasn't in the driver's seat. I didn't get to make the choices. What happened, happened."

"That's not good enough. That's not what I needed to happen. I needed you to do something heroic, to come and get us, to save us. Like always, you chose to do nothing," I said in a trembling voice. I wished I could have been stronger in the moment.

"Son, you aren't listening. There was nothing I could do," she repeated.

"If making your sons feel abandoned was beyond your control, then tell me about a choice you made over and over again." I swallowed deeply, not for effect, but in an effort to keep from screaming or crying. "Why did you keep sending Duke away?"

"Son, he was sick. He still is. You know that." I looked her straight in the eyes. I could see she was hiding something. I moved right next to her bed in hopes she'd see that I had no intention of settling for a pat answer, not today. Then out of the corner of my eye I saw a tiny green spider skitter across the windowsill.

I let out a war cry, "What the…I'm gonna kill your nasty ass," I leaped across the room and in a fluid motion removed a shoe and landed it squarely atop the small spider.

"My lord, son, it was just a tiny garden spider," Mama criticized.

"Spiders don't belong in the hospital. It's supposed to be clean and sterile in here. And you know good and well if I had my way I'd kill them all."

"It is clean in here. That tiny spider couldn't harm you if it wanted to. The thing probably came in with some of the plants or flowers," Mama said. For the first time the flora in the room registered with me. I had been literally focused on Mama looking so helpless in the hospital bed. There were a good many arrangements in the room. I pondered who cared enough to send flowers to this woman. As I mused, I could hear her saying how spiders were everywhere and I needed to move on and let them alone. A blinding moment of clarity crashed in on me. I had a lifetime of flashbacks. My

understanding became utterly clear.  How had I
missed it all this time?

"You're the spider!" I blurted out in a
glimmer of lucidity.  "I yell at you just like the
spiders before I kill them.  But I can't do anything
to you.  You're my mama."

"Son, what are you talking about?" Mama
asked, but I knew she understood.

"You!  You're the one.  I crush the spiders
because I can't crush you."

"You may as well give me your little hate
letter if all you are going to do is throw barbs."

"All these years I've been teed off.  I wanted
to...to... I've had to work, to run, to do anything
humanly possible to keep this beast inside me at
bay."

"I'm sorry for you and your brother, but
y'all aren't the first ones to be kin to violence, son.
My daddy whipped my ass just for not being a boy.
When I acted like a Tomboy trying to please him
he'd beat me and call me a fag.  To top it off your
sweet innocent grandmama would give me another
set of licks for making your granddaddy mad.  It
turns out that when daddy was mad at me he took
swings on mama, too.  The both of them drove me
to marry a man I hardly knew when I was just
teenager.  Then that miserable bastard thought he
could beat on me, too," Mama said without the
slightest tinge of emotion.

"You may not have beat on us, but you
punished us cruelly for nothing, for no reason at
all," I said.

"Son, you don't know cruelty.  Duke's
daddy and me would have knock down, drag out
fights.  After a spell he took to drinking and then we
really rumbled.  The police were out to our place

nearly every night. One night they came and broke it up the same as always. They should have taken one of us to jail. Later that same night he got tanked up and I took a baseball bat to the old sot and, well, that was the end of our fighting."

"What are you trying to say?" I asked, alarmed.

"You know damn well what I'm saying. I beat Duke's old man to death. So you need not come crying to me about your pain and what you have to do to keep your cool. I was raised by spiteful parents; the men in my life were sadistic and vicious. I realized it was in my blood when the two of you little thugs emerged from my own body. You're the smart one, so hear what I'm saying. This is our lot in life. Deal with it."

We sat quietly for a while. My cue to leave had come and gone. I fidgeted with the implements attached to her hospital bed. My involuntary movements got on my own nerves. I asked a stupid question.

"So that's why we never talk about him and why you sent Duke away?"

I hoped the silence would have afforded Mama a chance to think about her words and the tone she had used. Surely, she was feeling like she shouldn't have said all that stuff. Wrong again.

"Your brother is the spawn of a sorry and evil man. Of all the rotten luck, Duke looks just like his daddy. It makes me sick to be around my own firstborn. When I wasn't thinking about how nasty and vile his daddy was, Duke reminded me of the unspeakable thing I had done to his good for nothing drunk father. Who needs that mess around the house?"

I felt like I was talking to some hardened criminal. What happened to my lazy mother who hardly said a word? Mama read my seething. I tried to calm down and not overreact.

"How did you afford a lawyer good enough to keep you from going to jail?" I asked incredulously.

"Didn't need a lawyer. Not much came of the whole thing. Back in those days police reports were different than they are now. All the cops knew was that we were common trash. They had watched us fight many a time before. It was like a nightly ritual to have the cops pull that mother fucker off me. We were paperwork they didn't want to do."

"If you walked for that, why did you leave us hanging?" I demanded.

"No matter that the police turned a blind eye back then, I knew what had happened. And because of what I knew, I didn't want to make waves after I was arrested for the house. The prosecutor decided I was mentally imbalanced. He said no sane woman would live like that and keep children in filth. I didn't argue. The decision meant a halfway house over long term prison. I had one secret uncovered. My one big one remained concealed 'til now. I can live with that. I played the cards dealt to me and you need to pony up and do the same, little mister."

"Have you ever been happy?"

"Damn, son. This feel good stuff the doctors have put into you has made you less of a man than you used to be. Buck up, boy. If you came here for me to tell you something, then there it is. Buck up," she admonished.

"Jesus, now I'm afraid to ask you what became of my dad."

## Chapter 35

Play. Rewind. Play. Rewind. I practiced over and over the story I had for my session with Dr. Hayes today. It was true, and important. Most of all, it was my cover. At all costs I had to keep my visit to see mama under wraps. My open wounds still hurt. She had said way too much; it turns out the first cut isn't the deepest. I've got to avoid all that and be Mr. Happy-Go-Lucky. I entered Dr. Hayes' office with a smile.

"I'm feeling superb today. I've been looking forward to coming to see you," I announced cheerfully.

"I'm glad you're here and happy about it. What's got you in such a chipper mood?" Dr. Hayes asked me.

"I want to tell you about something silly from last weekend."

"Please do. Go right ahead." She relaxed her legal pad, put down her pencil, and looked on attentively.

"The Carpenters took me out to eat. We had a nice dinner. Afterwards we didn't go directly home; instead we drove out for a while. Dr. Carpenter exited the Interstate in Scottsdale. I know the area because I'd been there before visiting a girl. I thought we were getting gas at first, but we drove right past the service station at the intersection. We turned off the main road into a middle class neighborhood. I became very curious. I asked where we were going. Mrs. Carpenter told me to be patient. Seconds later the darkness of the winter evening sparkled, blinked and shone. Lights of all shapes, sizes and colors lined houses, trees, yards and fences. Lights were everywhere. It was

like the whole neighborhood was in a tacky
Christmas decoration contest.

"There were stars, Wise Men, Mary, big
Jesus, the baby Jesus and the other holiday icon,
Santa. I found myself smiling and asked why we
had come. They know I'm not big on Christmas
and the Carpenters are Jewish, you know. So I was
at a loss for an explanation. Mrs. Carpenter said she
didn't care about religious differences, she liked the
light show. She thought they were pretty, fun and
interesting in the political and religious statements
they made. She told me the two of them had been
coming to this same neighborhood for nearly a
decade. Over the years the light show had grown
bigger and bigger.

"Dr. Carpenter had us bent over with
laughter. At first he said if an alien landed it would
have no idea what to make of the lights or the whole
holiday season. Once he had us going he kept on
cracking jokes about the confusion with Saint Nick,
Santa Claus, Hanukkah, Kwanza, a terribly different
newborn and thirty three year old Jesus, multi-
colored lights, Christmas trees, three traveling
Persian astrologers, sleighs, wreaths, presents,
reindeer, snowmen, gifts galore and twenty four
hour shopping.

"We started up a hill. Dr. Carpenter drove
more slowly, not just for good viewing, but because
of traffic. The light show drew a crowd. We kept
rounding corners and saw more lights. Between the
lights and laughter I really began to enjoy myself.
We pointed out fascinating, creative and off beat
displays. My favorite was a shipwrecked Santa.
The jolly fat man sat in a grounded rowboat,
surrounded by beer crates and pink flamingos. He
was lit up like Las Vegas in more ways than one."

"Sounds like a very nice night," Dr. Hayes said.

"It was. What a nice night, indeed. We capped it off by stopping for donuts and hot chocolate at Krispy Kreme. Do you remember that I told you I don't celebrate Christmas?"

"Yes, but you never said why that is," Dr. Hayes said and adjusted her note pad so she could write.

"Canned corn. That's why I don't celebrate Christmas or Thanksgiving."

"I'm sure you plan to elaborate on that. Canned corn is not the answer I expected."

"It's the answer," I said. "When I was in grade school we had a food drive for the poor families. I begged my mama to let me take something in for the poor folks. I wanted to take canned corn. That was my favorite. I was sure some poor kid would love it the same as I did. Mama said to let it alone. I didn't. I snatched the corn one morning. In my rush I dropped it and dented the can. I figured it was good just the same. Mama walked in and caught me. She didn't say a word. I took the canned corn and hurried off to school. Later that week I got a box from the principal marked with mama's name. I took it home. I couldn't wait for her to open it. I proudly presented it to my mama when she got home from work. I'll never forget her opening it only to find my own dented can of corn! I stood confused, but the pained look on mama's face let me know what I feared was true. I knew in an instant that we were the charity case. I was crushed. I haven't eaten canned corn or celebrated a winter holiday since."

"Clearly, you had to know your family was in need," Dr. Hayes said.

"Clearly, you don't know what it's like for other people to know that about you."

"The point of the holidays is sharing and giving," Dr. Hayes pointed out.

"Even before the corn, I never knew how to accept gifts. I always felt guilty. I started thinking that people shouldn't spend money on me. I don't know how others feel when they get a gift. Maybe they don't have the same hang ups as I do. I also tend to worry about what if they don't like the gift. I'd be pissed off then after spending time and money to get a gift. I couldn't afford to give gifts as a kid and now I want to hold on to my money for fear of losing it."

"I hear you saying the holidays have been problematic for you in the past. Has that changed?" she asked.

"It's starting to change. That night with the Carpenters helped me to look past the cultural confusion, religious beliefs and commercial tyranny and see this time of year as fun and family focused. I felt happy. I liked it."

"I have to remind myself that you have had a long history in therapy to keep from being overwhelmed by your vocabulary and ability to be reflective."

"At least something good has come of all the misfortune of my life," I said.

"Your humor will help you, too," she said. "Don't let it go. You were happy to begin this visit. I've been pleased as well. I'm so glad you are finally bonding with the Carpenters. They are jewels of people. You are truly blessed."

"They are sort of neat. On the way home from the light extravaganza we talked about how Jewish families only have minimal decorations at

their homes for the holiday season, usually only a
menorah. We decided to change that and planned
how to decorate the house in a way that represented
us. We did it the next day. It was great. Our lights
and decorations represent each of us and pieces of
the world around us. Dr. Carpenter hung a big old
Star of David on the side of the house. Mrs.
Carpenter bought a three foot high illuminated
angel. I went for an empty manger. I strung lights
around its base and edges. It's a sight to see, a good
one. Looking at our representational religious and
personal electric art I realized there is a place for
me, even if it doesn't fit with the mainstream. No
matter what, it's out there. I really liked seeing my
understanding of Christmas in lights. I'll never
forget the Carpenters for that."

## Chapter 36

Among the many changes in my life, I had
stopped going to church. I regretted that choice.
Church had always been a source of conflict and
tension for me, but I longed for understanding about
the world around me and the life to come. I prayed
daily and read the Bible every once in a while. I
found that the passages jumped off the page and
said things in isolation that could drive a person
mad. But then one day I realized that I had spent
enough time alone. My loneliness ruled me and
warped my sense of the world. I wanted to be
someone who believed. I wanted to believe in
something bigger than all of us.

I set out to find a new church home. Mama
had found a new identity and surrounded herself
with people who cared for her in the church. The
warmth of the people who came to her memorial
service moved me in a way I had never felt before.
I gave thought to visiting that church, but it already
had history. I needed a fresh start. I made a list of
churches of all sorts of denominations and
systematically searched for a suitable place to join.
The most important thing I required was a change
from a theology of self-flagellation as a sinner. I
wanted to be a part of something and to engage in
the service of others.

After months of visiting churches I learned a
fair amount about evangelism. In an effort to reach
newcomers, churches sent out welcome packs with
information, cassettes of choir music and invitations
to meet personally with the pastor. Some churches
delivered cookies, fresh baked bread, cakes, pies
and homemade jams. I grew accustomed to the
goodies. Yet, some places only followed up with a

call or a letter and others did nothing at all. I appreciated the effort, but cared ultimately about what happened in the sanctuary.

One Sunday I skipped the church on my list and went to a service via invitation of a friend of an ex-girlfriend. I knew the girl I dated in high school had moved, so I went. It was unlike any service I had attended. They had incense, served wine to minors and the choir sat behind the congregation. Amidst all the new and unusual activities, I felt an openness that let me know I had found the right place. I had much to learn about these people and their traditions, but the pastor's sermon gave me confidence that this church would welcome me just as I was.

I filled out the visitor's card and requested a call from the Rector. Father Petrie called on Monday. We spoke frankly for some time. I liked him and the answers he gave about the church. He invited me to lunch and I accepted. Our table talk was better than the one on the phone. In an instant I preferred talking to him over Dr. Hayes. Maybe it was a gender thing, or maybe it was because it was my choice to talk with him, and not up to the courts. I didn't know for sure. I did know that I trusted him and in time I could be honest with Father Petrie. I discarded my list and have worshiped at that church ever since.

**Chapter 37**

Amazing Grace. How sweet the sound of
the powerful old song. It was grace that saved
wretches like us and mercy that allowed it to end.
I've been so lost, but now I find myself even worse
off, wandering around in the wilderness. I was
blind to the world around me and now I can see
more than I ever wanted, even through tears. I tried
to keep from crying during the moving spiritual. I
lost. The blasted third stanza said more than I was
ready to hear.

   Through many dangers, toils and snares...
   we have already come.
   'twas Grace that brought us safe thus far...
   and Grace will lead us home.

   It was the second time I had cried of late.
The best I could recollect, that doubled the amount
of times I had cried in my short life span. The last
time, like this one, was with my mom. I was a mess
as I left her hospital room. All the atrocious stuff
she said decimated the world I knew. My current
tears reminded me that we were both crying when
my mother last spoke to me. I was stomping my
way out of the little white room of horror and she
called to me. I refused to stop and listen.

   Mama had joined a church. I had no idea if
the people there knew much about her past. Mama
often said, "What you don't know can't hurt you."
It was that admonition that gave me the courage to
attend this service. I'm not sure knowing would
have mattered to the church members. These kind
and caring people visited with her. They came to
the hospital. It was their pastor who led this
memorial service. No one else from my family
came. I respectfully asked the Carpenters to let me

go this one alone. They always allowed me to drive the machine as it related to my biological family. I know they wanted to be there for me. Letting me be there alone meant the world and I'd never forget them for that. None of mama's old friends showed up either. Only a handful of the faithful from the congregation attended the service.

It was a nice way to remember and celebrate her life. As her closest living relative I had decisions to make. I had no experience in this area. I didn't know what to do, so I had her cremated. It was the least expensive of my options. In lieu of a casket a five by eight picture of mama sat on a small wooden table in the front of the church centered on the altar. I wondered who took the picture. We didn't have any family pictures or individual ones for that matter. I didn't have a single picture of anyone, not even myself.

I attempted to hurry away after the service. No such luck. I ended up in a makeshift receiving line in the parking lot. All these strangers offered the kindest of words about mama and encouragement for me along with hugs and prayers. I never felt so out of my element. I had to be careful not to mingle my thoughts with my words. The life that was being remembered was complex and colored.

When mama died she left no will, as she had nothing more to leave than a heritage. She left Duke and me as a harsh legacy of suffering. Among the mourners I saw Jane Boyd, the smoker I had met on the stairs of the halfway house where mama had lived. She approached without comment and handed me a note scribbled on folded sheet of paper from the hospital note pad. I read it and reread it after the parking lot parade was over.

You went on about writing a letter to me, so
I decided to write one to you. The main
reason is I left one of your questions
unanswered. Two things made me truly
happy in all these years. We had good times
at Scoping Point. I was happy there.
Believe it or not, the other is when I touched
you here in the hospital. I know it fell short
of a loving mother and son embrace. I can't
explain it, but those few seconds made an
old woman very happy. Thanks for coming
to see me. Thanks for listening. What I
passed to you that day was no worse than
what had already been done. Maybe the
knowing will make a difference. That was
the only day I can recall being completely
honest. It does help. It's one thing to talk
through all your problems. It's a totally
different experience to say it to someone
who understands and cares beyond an hourly
rate. Find someone, maybe that Julie of
yours, and be true to yourself. Hope is out
there. Don't sit around and wait for it to
find you.

Mama

At nightfall I drove to Scoping Point.
Somewhere between five and ten times mama,
Duke and I had come to this place. It's one the
highest points in the city. We'd pick up fast food
on mama's payday, drive up here, and look over the
lights of the big buildings in town. Mostly, though,
we'd stare at the moon, stars and other sparkling
things in the vast expanse above.

I got out, sat on the trunk of the car and
devoured a burger and fries. Since losing the
weight and living with the Carpenters I hadn't eaten
much in the way of fast food. The greasy fare
tasted nauseating and delicious all at once. I
remembered sitting in the very same spot with my
brother in the front seat and me always in back.
He'd take the carton with the most fries and pass me
whatever was left. I complained bitterly every time.
Mama would tell us to hush and we all ate and
watched the night sky, hoping upon hope to see a
UFO or shooting star, anything from the heavens.

The stars looked different now than when I
was a kid. Light and air pollution made them fuzzy
and distant. That's about how I felt. I knew that
like everything else, I had changed. I had changed
on the outside. I had lost weight. I took school
seriously and tried to learn something. I had a new
life, a new name and I wanted to believe I had hope.

The inside told a different story. In my head
I couldn't sell the story of hope. I only bought into
the reality of anger, self pity, self loathing and the
desire to be invisible. Inside I felt the curse that
flows in the blood of my family. I'm not sure if my
mother cursed me for all eternity, but I am certain
she made a decision to give me life. My brother
and I didn't do much or even symbolize happiness
for my mother during her life. In the exchange of
pain and misery the three of us gave as much as we
received and I'm satisfied to call it a draw. To even
the score, I knew that I could repay my mama for
the gift of life. I could give her rest and happiness.
I opened her urn. I placed my hand inside and
gently rubbed my fingers through the remains just
to touch her one last time. Then carefully and

quietly I spread her ashes under the starlit skies of
Scoping Point.

## Chapter 38

"Do you have lots of patients like me?" I asked Dr. Hayes.

"You know that I can't discuss my clients."

"If they're like me or not, you must have a good many clients. These are nice digs you have here. Oh, and by the way this new sofa is a winner. It's a sight more comfortable than the old one," I said, with a light bounce on the cushions. The old black one looked better than this one covered in a navy with a yellow rose pattern. That goes to show that looks aren't everything.

"I'm glad you like it."

"Back to your clients," I said. "The reason I asked about the other people you see is because I know how hard it is to live with all this nastiness in my head. The thing I don't know is why you would go to the bother of cluttering your head with the secrets of scary people."

Dr. Hayes studied me for some time before she answered. "I want to help. I can help you better if we talk about you rather than me and my practice."

I nodded in agreement and conceded, "Okay, here's an update for you. I joined a church and I'm seeing a new girl."

"You've been holding out on me," she said with a wry smile.

"I wrote about it in my journal," I crowed.

"Fair enough. I'd like to hear more. Tell me about the church first."

"Sure. You know I didn't feel right not going to church. I've gone to church on Sunday for as long as I can remember. I think that not going anymore is why I've been feeling hollow. I didn't get anything out of it when the Carpenters took me to the Synagogue with them. I liked the service. I know the Hebrew Bible pretty well and truthfully I like the stories better. But, I don't how to say this. The Christian service is what I'm more comfortable…well…I understand…I have heard about Jesus all of my life and that makes more sense to me. Do you know what I'm saying?"

"Yes, that makes perfect sense. Tell me about the church you're attending."

"Here's the short version. I wanted to go to a new church. I made a list of churches to visit. By a fluke I ended up at the Lutheran Church. Turns out that it's nearly as different from my old church as the Jewish service. The big difference is the communion. To Lutherans, that's the most important part of the service. They call it the Eucharist. I guess you probably knew that," I said. Dr. Hayes smiled and nodded as if for me to keep going.

"Anyways, the Eucharist and all is an experience of Jesus that's different than I'm used to and I sort of like it. I understand the Jesus in crisis, death and resurrection much better than the perfect, sinless, king of kings, prince of peace and savior of the world who will judge me on the last day. I find it hard to think about end times. I don't really want to think about it at all. But, crisis, that's where I live."

"Did you decide all that on your own or did someone spoon feed you the theological talk?" Dr. Hayes asked.

"Some of both. I've talked with the pastor a couple of times about the service and what it all means. And I can visualize myself and my place in the world through his sermons. That's what you are supposed to do, isn't it, listen and reflect?"

"Yes," Dr. Hayes said. "That's what most ministers hope for from their congregations. I look forward to reading your journal on this matter."

"When do I have to turn it in to you?" I asked nervously.

"It's not like a school assignment. There's no timeline or grade. I'll take it when you fill all the pages," Dr. Hayes said.

"Will I be done with it then?" I asked hopefully.

"No. I'll give you a new one."

"Oh."

"Let me say a word about your new church," She said frankly. "I know finding a church home is a daunting task. I'm glad you're happy, but I must share a concern I have. I'll be direct," she said and twisted to face me. "Your whole life has been about crisis and drama. At this point you are all but addicted to the stress and pain associated with them. Keeping that in mind I want you to consider that this may not be the best church for you."

"But I really like this church and the pastor is really cool."

"I didn't say stop going. I just want you to think about why you are there and what it is about the service that appeals to you. Give it a while. Write about it in your journal. I want you to take your time and be sure it's the right place and a healthy place for you."

"I hear you. I'll take it easy," I said, even though I didn't mean it. I don't think she believed my weak delivery.

"You mentioned a new girlfriend." Dr. Hayes said, indicating she wanted me to continue. I did as expected.

"She's not my girlfriend," I said. "We've been out a couple of times. It's no big deal."

"What's her name?" asked Dr. Hayes.

"Her name is Natalie," I said, trying to suppress a smile.

"Did you meet her at your new church?"

"No," I said. "We met in the grocery store. We've been hanging out mostly on the weekends. She's into the same music as I am. What can I tell you about her? Oh, this is funny. Natalie has these freaky friends and they go to the Rocky Horror Picture Show at midnight every weekend. Natalie's been like hundreds of times. She knows all the lines to the whole movie. They act out the parts and do all this weird stuff like talking to the screen and throwing junk during the movie. It's weird as all get out. Have you ever been?"

"I'm familiar with the movie."

"Okay, well then you know people dress up like the characters and sing along with all the songs and stuff. I didn't know about it. The first time Natalie took me I thought it was a side show for the night crazies. I'm not sure why, but I've been every Friday and Saturday for like the past four weeks.

"You've been to a new church, seeing a new young lady and going to a cult gathering for a month. Don't you think that's a lot for this to be the first time you mentioned any of it?" Dr. Hayes asked seriously. I hadn't told her about finding out that Duke's in jail, my regular contact with Bubba and I had skirted talking too much about mama dying. Just the thought of all that made me think that she was up to something. She's not a stupid woman. I tried to turn the tables on her.

"Hey now, I'm not the only one. You're holding out, too. You've never even blinked at any of the comments I've made since I've been coming to see you. At first I thought you had a ton of spooky patients and then I thought maybe you were a hard core professional. But today, I saw it when I asked you about your patients. Suddenly it made sense to me. You already had scary stuff rolling around in your head before you became a therapist. Something happened to you, something bad. I'm guessing this job is what you do to tame the creature."

Dr. Hayes offered no response. Once again she didn't even blink. She took no notes on the mystery pad. I took that as a confession.

"I know you aren't going to tell your story to me," I said. "Here's the thing. I need something to do, to make it better for me. I need to share my knowledge of the wickedness in a way that helps others who live with it, too. I'm hoping it will help me just as much."

"You are in the middle of treatment. You need to make yourself the top priority and the other will come," Dr. Hayes said.

"I can work on both at the same time. Here's something I wrote in my journal. I started by talking about a second hand Walkman I got from the flea market. Day and night I listened to the angst of John Mellencamp and Bruce Springsteen. I liked the lyrics Bruce and John wrote. They seem to feel the same as I do, but I can't help but to realize that their fame and fortune separates them from me and all the common folk. I finally made sense of it all. John Mellencamp and Bruce

Springsteen aren't necessarily posers who try to over relate to blue collar folks. They are who they are, and they can't help but to remember what that was like. Perhaps the memory hurts and haunts them the same as anybody. For them their music is a way to get it out. I can't play an instrument or carry a tune in a handbag, so what am I to do?"

As Dr. Hayes looked at me deciding what to say, I figured I was right. She knew a lot about life, way more than me. She wasn't going to tell me is what life had done to her behind closed doors. Among the many things this intelligent woman knew, I could tell she was acquainted with demons. Somewhere in the past she had come face to face with a demon of her own.

# Awakenings
## Chapter 39

"I had a freaky dream. Better yet, it was more like a nightmare," I said, and settled in the sofa a full sixty seconds or more before I uttered another peep.

"That's an interesting way to start our time together," Dr. Hayes said, causing me to begin shifting around in the corner of the sofa. She immediately noticed my nervous movement and tried to temper her comment. "Don't get me wrong. I want you to know I'm pleased you have arrived ready to work."

Her compliment made me uneasy. I felt kind of weird, as I recalled the many times I came into her office and took a seat with my arms strapped tight across my chest. I remembered feeling like I couldn't breathe because I was squeezing so hard. I found myself getting pent up and I decided it seemed like I was avoiding the process again as I sat silently thinking back on past visits.

Dr. Hayes prodded, "Was this a one time dream or is it a recurring dream that you have?"

"You know I have trouble sleeping a lot. I don't think I have ever told you about my regular nightmares. I have some of the same ones over and over, but I had this very creepy dream about a week or so ago."

"Is there a reason you want to talk about it now?" she asked.

"I don't know. Okay, well…yes," I said. "I didn't mention it sooner because I thought it's kind of silly to come here and talk about dreams."

"Some people take dreams very seriously," Dr. Hayes said. I could tell from her tone that she was not in that number. I decided not to say any more. I felt the warmth of my forearms wrapping around my midsection as I began to withdraw.

"I really would like to hear about your dream. Maybe it means something important."

I knew she was fishing, but I did want to try and figure out the disturbing dream and clear my head of it. So, I talked. "The reason I brought the dream up is that I keep having flashes of it in my mind. I remember it way too clearly. I really wish I could forget it, forget it all."

"Do you have a vivid recollection of the details?"

"Oh, yeah I do," I said. "I woke up with my face burning hot. I had sweated and completely soaked my sheets. It's haunting how well I remember everything about the dream."

"Will you tell me what happened?" she asked pleasantly.

"It's really kind of bizarre."

"It's very likely your dream is related to something going on in your life. I want you to know that working with dreams is not my forte, but I assure you whatever you have to say will be fine," Dr. Hayes seemed genuinely curious.

"Okay then." I scooted to the edge of the sofa and looked right at my therapist and told the tale, "In my mind's eye the entire scene replays in full color and sound. It went like this. I was sitting beside a very small pond. The water was dark and still. I don't know where this pond was supposed to be or why I was there. Woods surrounded the pond. In the distance I could hear something moving around in the woods. At first I ignored it. The crackling of leaves being crunched under foot got louder and louder.

"I spun to see what was coming out toward me. I have to admit that in the dream I was scared."

"Dreams are very personal and realistic. It's quite common to actually be afraid during and after a dream sequence," Dr. Hayes said.

"It wasn't just the movement in the woods. You see, where I grew up there was always a fear of a bad man in the woods because some crazy guy killed two boys about twenty years ago. He did it in the woods near the railroad tracks in my old neighborhood. The police caught the guy and he's been in prison as long as I have been alive. Still, my mama and other adults talked about the event like it could happen again at any given moment."

"Did a bad man come out of the woods in your dream?" Dr. Hayes said in an effort to draw me back on topic.

"No. Not at all," I explained. "A goose waddled out, followed by another. I assumed the two to be mom and pop as seven little geese trailed them out of the woods toward the small pond."

"Is there more to come? What you have said thus far doesn't sound so strange," she said, without looking up, as her hand busily wrote notes on her trusty yellow legal pad.

"Yes. There's more to come and the geese were the only normal part of the nutty dream. They moved along closer to the pond and cooed. Then suddenly two large, I mean unrealistically big dogs came bubbling up from the middle of the pond. Their enraged barks echoed. My first thought was not so much how did the dogs appear from the bottom of the pond as I worried about the baby geese. I thought for sure the dogs were after them."

"That's an admirable concern and quite normal to worry about the innocent," Dr. Hayes assured.

"I'm not finished yet. The dogs didn't go anywhere near the geese. The rabid dogs came straight for me with their mouths foaming and bearing their piercing teeth. Fear paralyzed me. I couldn't manage to move a muscle. My feet and legs felt like lead. In seconds the dogs pounced on me and began biting and tearing at my flesh. I don't remember feeling any pain from the dog bites as much as I felt like I was being ripped apart. I couldn't fight them off. Their teeth dripped with my blood," I said finishing my account of the dream.

"Is that all of it?" Dr. Hayes asked.

"Yes, that's it in all its weirdness."

"Steve, I must tell you that I don't pretend to proficient at analyzing dreams," she said. "In my training I studied the work of Carl Jung. He did a great deal of work with dreams and their interpretation. He suggested that our dreams utilized a shared pool of symbolism from mythology and religion. Jung thought these offered insights into the human psyche. With that said, most of what you have reported sounds like a textbook rendition of a struggle between good and evil. That's a battle I believe you know all too well."

"Yeah, I guess I've been to that dance a time or two. Here's the thing though. I mean. It's like...Well, you could say I believe in evil. Truth is, I know evil is in me. And that's it," I said trying to make sense to myself while talking. "I'm tired of being evil's whipping boy. Since I was a boy I've seen evil in the world all around me. I saw it in my home and I saw it inside me. To me that means evil really does exists. So, the way I figure it, on the flip side there has to be absolute goodness. There just has to be pure good in the world. There has to be a savior. I want that in my life. I want the good, not a combination of both."

## Chapter 40

"Are you all set to graduate?" Dr. Hayes asked, even though she knew the answer. As part of my treatment program I had to turn in copies of my report card to her along the way.

"Looks like I'm going to make it," I said. "But, I did get my first bad grade since I've been back in regular school."

"In which subject?" she asked.

"I had to complete a family tree for a project for my stupid social studies class. I didn't know what else to do so I made one using the Carpenters and their relatives. Once I got to school, I ditched it. I took the zero for the day. Turns out the project counted for twenty percent of the class grade. The teacher told me turning it in late was better than never. I stayed with the zero," I said. As I told Dr. Hayes about the incident I felt incredibly dim-witted.

"Why did you do such a thing?"

"Aw, you know. It's...well the Carpenters are good people and they've always been good to me, but I know we're really not family."

That sharpened pencil of hers would be dulled by the end of this session for sure. Dr. Hayes had been writing the whole time I talked about the family tree project. Presently she stopped talking and broke eye contact to write. Dr. Hayes generally wrote like a touch typist. She could write paragraphs without looking away from me. I often wondered if her words wandered outside of the margins. However the very straight row of sharpened pencils that lay ready on the side table and the ever clean and organized desk of hers suggested that Dr. Hayes wrote neatly between the lines and within the margins, even without looking.

"You don't have to be blood relatives to be family," she told me, as if I didn't know.

"I know that. Duke has a different daddy and he's my brother."

"Yes, that's true," she said. "The same bond is there for adoption, marriages and…"

"Marriage is not an option," I said interrupting Dr. Hayes. "I can handle having just one girlfriend. When I get older I might live with a girl, but I'm never getting married," I stated firmly. I had gotten good enough that I could tell Dr. Hayes had only written one word on the yellow legal pad this time. I'm sure that word was "marriage."

"When do you want to talk about the girls?" Dr. Hayes said while making very intentional eye contact.

"What about them? I like girls. I date them."

"Why do think that is?" Dr. Hayes asked.

"I don't like being alone. Girls are the easiest way to take care of that."

"Is that all there is to it?" she asked.

"No, it's not. I've already said I like girls, lots of them. It's not all me. Turns out the girls I date have needs, too."

"That doesn't sound like you talking. You're long past blaming others. So, am I to believe you are regressing or is there something that you're just not saying?"

"I'm sure there's some baggage you want me to unpack," I said sarcastically.

"Yes, but I'm not sure what's happening here. You're not usually so snippy."

"We both know that I choose not to stay in relationships."

"True enough. What I need you to acknowledge is why that is," Dr. Hayes said.

I gave in and started talking to drown out her rapidly-writing pencil. Never before had Dr. Hayes taken so many notes. "Okay. Here's what you want to hear. Back when I was a fat boy, I hated myself on the inside. I thought if I liked what I saw on the outside I'd feel better. All it did was cost me money for new clothes. Since I lost the weight, got a little confidence and picked up some psychological tips from the Carpenters, I found that I can nearly smell a lonely girl. I'm like a predator. They make me feel good about me. Girls help me to forget about life for awhile and escape to some fantasy place of happiness."

"That sounds like something an alcoholic might say to justify drinking," Dr. Hayes said.

"I'm just being honest about what I do and why."

"You need to know that your actions and what you have said in response to them are tantamount to addictive behavior."

"You know good and well I'm clean," I said. "I'd never even consider dope. A boy in the group home once told me that just one little hit of the rock and it will own you forever. I'm not about being a slave to anything."

"Steve, we've talked about addictive behavior before. It's not only about drugs and alcohol. You know that."

"Is it so wrong to want to feel good for a change?"

"We all have ways of self-medicating. Is that all it's about for you, feeling good for a brief period of time?" she asked.

This topic amounted to a big old can of worms I didn't want crawling around. I knew eventually we'd have to talk about control issues. In response, I tried to control the conversation. "Do you really want to open this cage? I'm tired of telling you I need to channel all the stuff inside of me. Here's what I know," I said. "I can't volunteer to mentor troubled kids. That's too close to home. Hospitals won't work either. Dying people are too damn honest. I need to let a little beauty, a little goodness in my life. Girls are as close as I can get, but the truth is they don't really take care of it for me. Like I said, I know I'm a predator. To be with girls for me is feeding, not healing. I'm tired of longing. I want to belong," I admitted.

"I hear you when you say that and I've heard you when you mentioned it before. I want you to think about the fact that you already belong more than most people. You have a family and an adopted family. Where is it you want to belong? Everybody has felt pain. What makes you think you are so different?" Dr. Hayes asked.

That question pissed me off. "I'm damned," I responded. "I'm not different. To answer your question, it's desperation that sets people like me apart. I think you know something about that. If you're still being professional and pretending that you aren't taming a fiend of your own, then here's how it's different. To me desperation is being afraid that you will freeze to death in your own bed. It's not being able to drink water in your own house. It's a girl selling her ass at seven in the morning because she has nothing else of value.

Desperation is the desire to kill a mother fucker
when nothing else will suffice."

Dr. Hayes set aside the legal pad and said,
"You have developed survival skills beyond
civilized instincts. Regardless of your crude
methodology, you made it. While navigating years
of abnormal situations you inadvertently merged
punishment and values as your standard of
normalcy. You experienced change and continuity
and learned that adaptation is essential to survival.
In this concept form follows function."

"I have no idea what you are talking about,"
I said honestly.

"In short I'm saying that for every action
there is a reaction, and that you have worked that
out in a way that has a lot to do with guilt and
acceptance of the belief that you are less than
worthy," Dr. Hayes said.

"In whatever it is you just said are you
telling me that I give credit to the sire who turned
me out? That my life is full of decay because I was
raised in a landfill?" I asked, seeking clarification. I
realized that somehow she had taken control of the
conversation.

"No. I'm not giving you an option to place
the blame of any part of your life on anyone else.
I'm saying that you take what happens to you and
internalize it all, the good and the bad."

"So, for example, when I was in grade
school I got a daily punishment of sitting in an open
locker with my shirt collar on a coat hook. As an
added measure, I got a mouth full of what we called
'hot stuff' for cussing or talking back to teachers. I
later learned the hot stuff was Listerine. To this day
I rinse with it in the morning and before bed."

"You've got it," Dr. Hayes said. "I want you to think about that sort of thing. Write in your journal about it. We have a lot of work to do in this area."

"Before I leave for the day let me make sure I'm on track. Does this fit with what you are talking about?" I asked. There was a health center on the same property where I went to elementary school. Occasionally, I'd try to buck out of class by complaining of a toothache so as to go down to the dentist. My third grade teacher knew my teeth didn't cause me any pain. She used to say, 'Boy you a lie and the truth's not in you. Jesus makes no room for liars in heaven.' For reasons unknown to me, after her mini-sermons, she'd send me off to the dentist. If I had to guess, I think she let me go to get me out of her hair for awhile.

"On the way to the health center I always made a side trip through the woods down a steep muddy hill to a small creek. After I'd played around for a while, I'd finally stumble in to the health center. It seemed as though the dentist always found a cavity or two. I used to think that getting the cavities filled was Jesus' way of punishing me for lying and wasting time at the little creek."

I thought about what I had just said and decided I had answered my own question. "You're right. That's the way it is with me."

## Chapter 41

Tap. Another droplet of perspiration dripped from the nape of my neck and landed on the sheet. The pungent musk of my sweat-stained mattress took me back to the old days. Sleeplessness, my old friend, had returned. I would have much rather had my buddy, MD, back in my life. Really, it would be good to see a familiar face once and a while. Just thinking of MD and all the time we spent and the goofy stuff we did together reminded me of happier times. It felt good to smile. It only lasted for a minute as this stupid journal reminded me that it was that time in my life I'm now led to believe warped me.

So, here I am at no o'clock in the morning reminiscing and making a legitimate entry in this journal. I'm still not certain what I think or how I feel about mama's hospital bed confession. In many ways, I'm not overly surprised. There were times when she would give Duke and me looks and we knew that if we didn't comply with her demands, she'd inflict a world of hurt on us. I took it in stride that my grandparents and mama lived the same hostilities that Duke and I wrestled with for as long as I can recall. It's what we do. It's who we are.

Mama never did say why she was in the hospital. She looked like shit. I knew at the time that whatever she had, it was killing her. I got that from the simple fact that she didn't offer to tell me about it. I didn't bother to ask anyone at the hospital. For old time's sake I decided to ignore it. I didn't want to know. On the way home from the hospital I wondered who from our neighborhood knew the truth about what mama did. I couldn't

figure how they managed to keep silent about a
woman beating her husband to death. Jesus, they
gossiped about everything under the sun. Wait a
minute. Now I get it. Oh my god, that's worse.
They did talk. I'm sure they talked a lot, just not to
me.

The journal doesn't know, but I put down
my pen and laid in the bed for over an hour. I
didn't manage to fall asleep, so here I am again. I
guess I should write about the thoughts swimming
through my head. Lying in bed awake reminds me
of living in the group home. Night after night there
I feigned sleep as a protective measure. Keeping
one eye open was not nearly enough to be vigilant
against physical or sexual attacks. Every single
night I prayed to whoever would listen. I placed my
soul on the auction block. I offered to trade my soul
and faithfully serve God, Satan or whoever could
remove me from the pit that was my life.

I never had a road to Damascus experience,
which led me to believe that like my life, my soul
was of no value. That didn't stop me. Nightly, I
went through the ritual of praying for relief. It
never came. All that happened was Eggie Baby.
He came without fail to remind me I was already in
Hell.

Once he came in the middle of the night. I
had opened the bidding on my soul. The usual lack
of interest from the powers that be set the tone for
another sleepless night. Then Eggie Baby made his
move. I don't know what he was thinking because
he came alone. He threw a blanket over me and
then punched and kicked me. I wrapped around
him and took him to the ground. Once I had seized
the upper hand I laid him out on his stomach and
pressed my knee in his back.

I had fought this little thug long enough to know that nothing would satisfy him until he killed or maimed me. My only other option was to kill him first. I fumbled with my mattress and found the slit in it. I dug around and fished out a razor I had stolen from an annoying punk some weeks previously. I took it and carved my initials in Eggie Baby's shoulder. As I tattooed him I told him how he couldn't see my initials, but like the scar that would remain, I'd forever be close by and he should always be looking over his shoulder, as the next time I meant to kill him.

I let him go and he went berserk. Immediately I knew my poetic threats were lost on him. I went with Plan B. Without hesitation I put the full force of my heel on his knee. It buckled backwards like a camel's. A grotesque crackling sound preceded his animalistic cry of pain. He went down in a sniveling heap.

Even though he was in my room after hours, the whole ugly matter got me busted down to Day One, Level One. It took a month or so until I made it back to general population. I saw Eggie Baby in the cafeteria. Instead of trying to kill me with a threatening look, he diverted his eyes. From then on the he let me alone. I believe that night I took Eggie Baby past the idea of pain and etched it as a living memory and that's why he never came for me again.

Recalling my own brutality brought it home. It all made sense to me more than ever before. My whole family had been bound by blood and behavior to a life of violence, pain and uncertainty. I remembered her words: "After our third date a goodnight kiss didn't do the job. He raped me." Mama had said the last sentence in baby talk. It was the one time I can recollect when her self-control lapsed.  As real as what happened to her was, she still removed it from it in actuality.

Regardless of her delivery of the statement, I couldn't believe what she had said.  More than that, I couldn't believe she had said it, not to me.  I couldn't believe that in every possible aspect I came to this life in a vacuum of revulsion.  Prior to that revelation from mama, I thought I knew and had lived the unbelievable.  In that moment mama visited a new and excruciating reality on me.  What was she thinking?  I was just a kid; why treat me like a man?

What doesn't make sense is why it had to be that way.  In school I was given tools to interpret poems, literature, and art.  In Sunday School and Church I was taught to interpret the Bible.  Newspapers and talk shows told me how to interpret politics.  Shouldn't there be somebody out there to help me interpret life?

It's sure as hell not professionals in the psychological field.  All the therapists I have had to deal with have made me dig up the past and talk about how that makes me feel.  None of them, not one, tried to make sense, rationalize or at least make an attempt to harmonize why people do the things they do.  All I have done to date is trot out my shortcomings and the mistakes of my family like a grotesque parade or carnival.

Prior to all the professional help of late, I was blissfully unaware of my misery.  My custom-made blinders worked just fine.  Once my eyes were opened to the all that existed around me, I quickly determined I preferred the world where I knew less and hoped for more.  Now, I'm acutely aware of my pain.  I want to know why it happens.  Is it

unexplainable?  I need an answer.  Will my pain
ever end?  When will it end?  It's not okay for it not
to end.

I have to find some happiness.  I have got to
change my destiny.  God help me.

## Chapter 42

"Can I ask you an odd question?"

"Don't be silly. You can ask anything, but I may give an odd answer," Father Petrie said with a slight chuckle.

"The Bible talks about dreams all the time. Do you think that dreams mean anything?" I asked.

"Yes, the Bible does mention dreams a good bit, but they aren't always the same as the dreams we think of when we use the same word. But to answer your question, yes. I took several classes on the brain and human behavior. I believe dreams are very important and can have significant meaning."

"In your classes did you learn how to interpret dreams?"

Father Petrie chuckled at my question. "Dreams, like the Bible, are open for interpretation. Conventions and standard ideas for interpretation exist, but they vary widely. My professor used to tell us the mainstream theories, followed by his theory if it was different, but then he'd always say, 'The truth is, we don't know.' Again, the long answer is that I know some traits of dreams but I can't tell you that they are one hundred percent Gospel truth."

"Okay," I said, and decided not to go any further with it.

"Are you going to tell me your dream or not?" he asked.

I caved because I really wanted to talk about it. "I had a dream where I was sitting in the lobby of my therapist's office," I corrected and continued, "when over the loud speaker I heard the receptionist call for help in Dr. Hayes' office. She said there was a ghost in the room. Instinctively, I got up and

ran to help. I felt sure I had misheard the ghost part,
or that 'ghost' was an interoffice term for 'patient
gone wild.' As I opened the lobby door I suddenly
felt overly gallant. I decided to go back to my seat
and keep reading a magazine. Before I turned back
I noticed other doctors and employees closing their
doors. No one was going in to help Dr. Hayes. So,
I ran to her office. She had moved rooms and let a
new therapist in the practice have her old office. I
rushed through the door to find her behind her desk,
a place where she never actually sits. She had a lot
of kids in her office. It was like group therapy or
something. The small and narrow room was
cramped. I hurried behind Dr. Hayes and felt
something corporeal. I panicked. It dawned on me
that ghosts really did exist.

"I found myself wrestling with the ghost. I
called out to one of the kids to get pencil shavings
from a sharpener mounted on the wall. Before the
girl could get to me, I released the ghost. I
immediately made the sign of the cross, blessed the
ghost and began saying prayers. The group of kids
kept asking Dr. Hayes what I was doing. The ghost
left, or at least I felt its presence leave. I whispered
to the little girl to keep the pencil shavings, as if the
ghost couldn't hear me. I remember being very
conscious of that."

"Why did you want the pencil shavings?"

"I planned to throw them on the ghost so I
could see its form."

"Good idea. I was confused by pencil
shavings being in a psychologist's office," he said.

"Dr. Hayes always used a pencil with her
big yellow pad. She always kept an ultra sharp
point on the pencils. She must have had a sharpener
somewhere."

"Are you familiar with the story of Jacob wrestling with the angel of the Lord?"

"Yes. Jacob was lucky. He got the blessing."

"Along with a broken hip," Father Petrie added.

"If that was all that was at stake, I'd take that deal. Can you tell me anything about the dream?"

Father Petrie nodded and laughed out loud for the third time. "Keep in mind this is not cast in concrete. I'll tell you what my professor would have said about your dream. First, you have a deep and abiding respect for Dr. Hayes. You show that in two ways. One is you wanted to help her. The other is you represented her as generously giving up her room and taking a smaller one to make room for a new colleague. The small and narrow room itself means you are feeling constricted or smothered. It symbolizes the walls closing in on you. The ghost in the dream represents an unresolved issue in your life. Your concern with the pencil shavings can be thought of as a desire to uncover the mystery of the issue or maybe you wanted to know what she wrote about you."

"Bingo! Give the dream weaving pastor a prize! I often thought of breaking into her office to read the notes on her pad. I could have, easily. The building had little league security system."

"What kept you from doing it?' he asked.

"I guess I did respect her, and I've learned that there are some things I really don't want to know."

"Like the unresolved issue you may or may not have?"

"Unresolved issue. You have no idea," I said. Without even thinking, I opened up and moved from the dream and told Father Petrie about the nightmare of my life. He listened as if rather than a tale of garbage, spiders and hostility; I was recounting the most important epic in the history of time. He had a good way of being present and making me feel important.

When I finished I felt bad for dumping on him, and the hour was late. I felt for sure I had stayed long past my welcome. I moved to leave. We stood at the same time. Father Petrie said, "The blessing and prayers. That's interesting."

"Is that all?" I asked inquisitively.

"For now," he said, rubbing his chin and intentionally looking pensive. "Let me remind you this not an exact science. I'd be negligent not to repeat what else my professor would say."

In concert the pastor and I stated, "We don't know."

## Chapter 43

I have no doubt that if I counted, anger would be the word that appears with the most frequency in this journal. It's funny. I haven't picked this thing up in a while and the first thing I have to write about is the same old crappy crap. I'm sick of it. My fucking anger is burning a whole in me deep enough to traverse Hades. I have to close it. I've got to find something to fill it. Fighting, girls, money, the Carpenters, nothing does it for me. Nothing is good enough to make me completely forget. None of those things make me feel any better about my life. All of my regular outlets for self-medicating hold any currency for me, not anymore. I need something new. I need to change my ways, to do noble things.

It's been a month or so since I've thought about this. I finally got back around to writing. I think it makes the most sense to continue this entry. The day after I wrote the paragraph above I arranged to meet with Father Petrie, the pastor at my church. I was still new to the church at that point. I spared him the horror of my story and instead filled him with a line that I wanted to spend a year or two in community service prior to attending college. He bought it.

It turns out that Father Petrie had taken a year off and traveled to Spain before he went to college. Fate had it that my white lie resonated with the pastor. He put me in touch with Gloria, a parishioner at the church, who had recently received a grant to begin a holistic treatment program. She planned to open three transitional houses for homeless men. She had money to fund three positions. That sounded like a perfect fit for what I needed, where I was and who I am.

I looked at it like this. I was alive. My mom gave me life. My adopted parents gave me a chance. I took advantage of both and much like the Carpenters I wanted to give something back. I had just finished high school and didn't have any desire to go to college, much to the Carpenters' dismay. I just wanted to do something.

## Chapter 44

"Father Petrie gave you a ringing endorsement, and based on our conversation today I feel comfortable offering you the job. The only thing I need to do is to have a background check completed. It's no big deal. We all have to do it as a stipulation of the grant. At your age, you can't have anything to hide," Gloria said.

I froze. A background check? A movie of the bad and illegal things I had done in my life played in my head. I knew that all of my offenses had happened as a juvenile and all of the mess with mama's house had been suppressed by the courts. I still felt a little uneasy. I knew Steve Mallory had nothing to hide. The problem came as I had nothing to show. As Steve Mallory, I had no history. As that person, I just appeared on the planet a couple of years ago. Like Melchizedek, who I had learned about from Father Petrie, my new persona existed without father or mother, without genealogy, without beginning of days or end. It was unto its own and would remain as such forever.

"I want you to go ahead and start work," Gloria informed me. "It may take a while for the background check. I've been told that a private investigator or security firm can do the checks for us. I haven't found anyone to do it as of yet."

"Hey, I know a guy," I said eagerly. "He's a private investigator. His name is JT Cook. He's good. You've probably seen him on TV. He's had some important cases."

"Oh, if you could put me in touch with him, that would be perfect," Gloria said. "Father Petrie was right. You are a good one."

What a break. I called the investigator, trying to remember what name he called me. He didn't know me as Steve, for certain, but was I Fat Boy to him? Or something else? I had met JT Cook when I was in middle school. One day after school, Bubba, MD and I played Silo, Caddie, and Paul in a game of football in a side yard. I remember getting tackled by Caddie. As I looked up and wiped dirt and grass from my face I noticed a blue Pacer parked on the street. My first thought was, what an ugly car! My second thought was, what was a guy doing driving such a sissy car? A guy I didn't recognize sat in the driver's seat. The guy had a handlebar mustache. It was the first one I had actually seen. It looked pretty gay to me. We continued playing ball.

After a while I realized the strange guy was still parked in the same place. In the last couple of weeks we had a pervert riding around asking boys if they needed a ride. Unfortunately for him, he tried it with some kid on a rare day Duke was home. I saw a boy I knew from school get in the car with the sleaziod. I started yelling, "That's him. That's the perv!"

Duke ran over to the car and started kicking the driver's side door. The boy got out and ran as Duke instructed. The dude pulled away. I threw a rock. I was no Silo. I didn't do any damage, as my stone landed on the back bumper of the compact car as it hurried away.

I thought that had been the end of such things, until this weirdo sat across the street watching a bunch of boys playing football. Pretending to be in a huddle, I pointed him out to the other guys. Then I slipped off. I cut across yards, and came up on the opposite side of the car.

The guys made a ruckus to act like they were fighting over the game and I bum rushed the car.

The man in the car found our sneak attack very amusing. He let us know he was a private investigator. He showed us his identification. That didn't do much for me. I had seen similar badges in kids' magazines. We took to believing him after he told us that he was there doing surveillance on Mrs. Skylar. Her husband suspected her of cheating on him.

The investigator told us all kinds of tales about his previous adventures. I took most of them to be completely made up for our amusement. He was a great storyteller. I stayed after the other guys had to go home for dinner.

"Mrs. Skylar is doing it with someone other than her husband, but she never does it here," I said knowingly.

"What makes you so smart?" the investigator questioned.

"Simple. She comes to every practice and every single game. Then she lets her son go home with his friends and she hangs around. It's all very nicely done. From the outside you'd think she's a super mom. I don't blame her for getting some strange."

"Why's that?" JT asked.

"What's so funny is that her old man, the one that hired you, he's banging a girl that goes to the high school. They always make it under the power lines. We go and watch them sometimes."

JT and I got along great. Over time, I proved to him the antics of both Mr. and Mrs. Skylar. I don't know for a fact, but I feel certain he worked that one from both sides to his monetary benefit. After that, JT put me to work. I did a bunch of silly little things like take pictures, watch houses and deliver packages. I sometimes enlisted the help of my buddies, but they had no idea I was working, much less getting paid. JT gave me ten dollars an hour. Those were big bucks to a kid in those days.

     "Hey. You know who this is?"

     JT responded, "Of course I do. Are you ready to do some work for me?"

     "I'll be happy to help you out. I can use the cash, but first I need you to do a little something for me," I said.

## Chapter 45

After the very informal, yet nerve racking, interview with Gloria over a glass of iced tea following church, I immediately went work as a program assistant. I discovered that was a nice title for worker bee. I liked it from the get go. From what I knew about social work it seemed to me there was an obvious rush to care for women and children, so I liked the idea of working with the guys. Truthfully there's a sociologist in me who wanted to learn about why so many men in our society make bad choices involving sexual abuse, drug and alcohol abuse and violence.

When JT agreed to handle the background checks he encouraged me to pick up a hand gun. Nothing big, he said, as he warned me that a day might come when the element of surprise would come in handy and do more service than a bullet. I was assigned the smallest house. Right out of the gate I found myself working with one particularly rowdy group of guys. I was glad I had listened to JT. False security or not, I liked having options.

Gloria, the woman in charge, handled the largest of the houses. She was a mountain of a woman. I didn't think she needed a gun or any other weapon for that matter. My beautiful and intriguing coworker, Susannah, managed the third house. She had a much more delicate frame and I often had concerns about her safety in this brutal environment. There'll be more to follow on Susannah in a separate journal entry, hopefully several more.

Gloria's master plan placed all of our participants in rehab programs. We partnered with a vocational tech school and offered training

courses for carpentry and construction. Participants
in the program were issued food stamps, weekly bus
passes and provided with clothing. The plan was
perfect. Execution, well that was something
different. We tried to keep them busy with a full
load of work, study and treatment to keep the guys
off the streets and out of trouble. The biggest
obstacle came from the drug trafficking of the
neighbors. The house that I work with sat between
competing dope dealers. Business was good. The
two drew a never ending stream of novice and
experienced buyers. I remember when a car load of
teenaged white kids came down looking for trouble,
the kind they know nothing about. I overheard an
interaction.

"I'll take one," a nubile girl said,
presumably meaning one rock of crack form
cocaine.

My all time favorite came after two days of
ice and snow. It was about seven in the morning
and some hard up druggies made two passes of the
slush covered street. A haggard dude rolled down
the window and yelled to me, "Hey, are they open?"

With all the drugs and violence I quickly
likened the experience of working with the guys to
being in the group home, but with much bigger kids
and bigger problems. Along with less than fond
memories, I soon began to have headaches and
wanted to quit. These guys connected to an awful
thing in me. We all related to one another even
though I was considerably younger. The insight
helped me to know who was scamming, who was
laying up in the house all day, who was drinking,
selling dope, the whole thing. From the get go I had
no problem busting them down. It was the right
thing to do. It was power. It was control I had

never known. We worked on brutal honesty. If you were caught you got called out. If you were caught again, you were thrown out.

Any given day somebody disappeared. The guys went on binges and then tried to come back. That's not how we operated. The welcome mat got pulled. If a guy refused to leave then I had to call the police on him for criminal trespass. Once I came by and found a fellow slumped over. I thought he had passed out. No, he had overdosed and had been dead for a couple of hours, or so the medical examiner said.

I had asked to work in the community. I got what I wanted, and all its nobility. Somehow I knew this was not what Rhonda made me promise to do.

## Chapter 46

"Damn, boy. I hardly even recognized you."

"It's good to see you, too," I said to my brother. He sat across from me in a prison issue faded orange jump suit. Duke held a phone receiver pushed to his shaven head.

"Don't be an ass. You're... You ain't fat anymore," Duke said.

"Yeah, and you're baldheaded."

"I said don't be an ass. Since you're not a blubber butt anymore; what cha' you reckon I should call you nowadays?" he asked.

"Fat Boy's all right with me. I'm used to it. How about I start calling you Mr. Clean?"

"Keep on and you're gonna piss me off," Duke said. "For real, I feel retarded calling a little boney ass like you Fat Boy."

"Don't sweat it, Duke. I'm just a couple of cheese burgers, fries and a milkshake away from gaining it all back. Life all the time slaps you back down. You know that."

"Dude, you need to lighten up. I'm the one on the wrong side of the locked door here. You should be living large with your skinny self. I bet you got all kind of honeys nowadays," he said, as if I was human girl repellant before.

"I know I was no Casanova, but I did okay and had plenty of girlfriends before I lost the weight," I protested.

"You know that's right, you were no Casanova. You were more like a Romeo Void--a fat one," Duke joked.

"Damn, I'd prefer a beating from you than this."

"I'm just joshing your little boney ass," Duke said.

"Stop it with the boney stuff," I said. "I told you I like Fat Boy better. That's who I've been most of my life. My shrink says seeing myself as fat is part of my physical identity. I think it's an identity crisis. I've been a lard ass forever. Without a mirror, my mental picture of myself is the same two hundred pounds it ever was."

"Spare me all that head talk. I get enough of it in here. All these mother fuckers think they're a doctor or a lawyer just 'cause they read a book."

"Ah, the old jailhouse university, huh?" I said.

"You know it. Tell me, what are you doing with yourself nowadays? I hope you're in school. You were always book smart," Duke added.

"Naw, man. I went to work."

"Doing what?"

"I'm working with these guys in a transitional program."

"What the fuck is that?" he asked.

"We help homeless guys get into drug and alcohol treatment, job training, housing, therapy. That kind of stuff," I said.

"What's up with the good citizen routine? Did your 'shrink' put you up to that? You need to come clean and admit it won't do no good. What do you think helping the homeless is going to do?" Duke asked with a laugh.

"Nothing much. I'm just trying to do something right for once in my life," I said.

"Boy, it don't matter what you try to do now. It's all been done. You're a hard headed heathen. There ain't no good in you. You and me, we're both goin' straight to Hell."

"Thanks for your support," I said.

"Boy, I'm gonna bust your smart mouth. Look, I'm still not sure what to make of your skinny little ass. What's got me rattling even more is; why are you here?" Duke asked with a piercing stare.

"Do you know mama died?" I said.

Duke gave no indication that he heard me or cared whatsoever about what I said.

"Did you hear me? Did you hear what I said?" I asked.

"Were you with her when she went?"

"No, but I did see her in the hospital before she went. She asked for you."

"Liar," Duke said. "I know better. She's our mama. We ain't supposed to forget that, but we don't have to care about her." I could tell he did, no matter what he said. I took the opportunity to change the subject.

"Dude, you were right. The boys in the group home took pain and misery to new heights."

"You should've listened to me sooner," he said.

"Let me ask you a question. How did you manage being in that place? How did you live being locked up with those freaks?

"I stayed high to protect myself," Duke declared. "That's what I did."

"How did you get the dope in an institution?"

"The same way I get it in here," he said. "You do what you have to just to get by."

"Aren't you afraid of getting busted and getting your sentence extended?"

"Don't worry your skinny little self. Tell me, how'd you find me?" Duke asked.

"I've got my ways. You know I always said I'm a man of means."

"Stop it with the cool talk," he said. "You should have just admitted Bubba told you."

"He didn't," I protested.

"Seeing how I got here while his daddy was polishing off the last two months of his sentence, my guess is Bubba's the only one who you're likely to hear from."

"The old street savvy comes through again. Do you know what the Pythagorean Theorem is?"

"You seemed to have forgotten who you're talking to," my brother said in a furious tone.

"What's up with all the hostility?"

"Looks like your book smart savvy fails once again. You don't get it, do you?"

"I guess not. Enlighten me."

"Oh, Jeez. Enlighten? You're lucky this plate glass is between us. I'll enlighten your ass all right. Look boy, we both know we ain't supposed to be together. We're dangerous seeds in turbulent ground. Our miserable lives have been bound by a tragic thread that's ready to snap," Duke waxed poetically.

"We're brothers. That's what we are. We're all that's left of our family," I said.

"You're killing me with this sensitive talk. It's not our style. Let it go. Let the whole damn thing go. Look at yourself. You caught a break. You're out of that fucked up house and out of trouble. Check you out, Fat Boy. You're sitting up here looking good. Keep it going and you keep going. Don't look back and don't come back," Duke paused. "I don't want to see you again unless you are on TV doing something special."

"Stop being stupid, Duke. I spent my whole life trying to be with you. Now that we're old enough, no one can stop that. I can visit you here. Once you get out you can bunk with me. I'm going to get my own apartment. I can't afford much, but can bet your ass it will be clean."

"How sentimental. You're not my keeper and you're not listening to me. I spent my whole life staying away from mama, that house and you. We got bad stuff in us, boy. You might be able to pretend it's not there. I can't. Listen to this boy, we are where we are. I did all I can for you. You learned how to survive didn't you? That was all I could do. I can't take part in the rest."

"Say what?" I said, genuinely confused.

"I don't want to be the one who takes you off the leash," Duke said, brashly.

"So this is it?" I asked in a shaky voice.

"Do you want to end up in a place like this?" he waved his hand behind him. "Do you want to be in here with me? Do ya? You didn't listen about the group home. That's not even the warm up act of what will come of us if we're together. We're Satan and Damien. Dig this, little brother, your skinny ass and fancy talk won't get you nothing up in here 'cept a boyfriend. So straighten up and stay clean."

"Stop it," I said tearfully.

"Don't be a sissy," Duke said. The phrase took me back in time. I flashed back to the countless times he had said that to me. It was never an insult. It came as a gentle prod and it always worked. Today would be no different. Duke painfully pulled me back into the present.

"This is it. I'm sorry you had to come here for me to let you down again. But it is what it is," he said with no hint of remorse.

I jumped up and punched the glass divider. It didn't buckle. My fist immediately began to trickle blood. I screamed, "Fuck you!"

Duke dropped the phone on the desk and called for the guard. He walked to the door and turned back to me. He mouthed, "I love you, too."

## Chapter 47

Day one as a full time employee I had to unload furniture into the three houses. I arrived at the first house a few minutes early. The site caseworker greeted me.

"Hi. You must be Steve. I'm Susannah," she said while extending a hand. After pleasantries she informed me the two of us were the moving crew for the day. She pointed to a loaded moving truck in the driveway. We made a great team. We talked as we labored and sweated. I learned she was from Cuba. She told me how her family had made a courageous voyage across the ocean to the United States.

For a thin woman with a small frame she could hold her own while heaving tables, sofas and chairs, oh my! Maybe that came from harrowing days of keeping her head above water. The two of us made quick work of filling up the houses. I immediately grew fond of her no nonsense attitude. Jeans and a tee shirt made sense for hauling furniture, but her sandals seemed less than practical. The more I listened to her I decided she was like that every day, regardless of the work she was doing. Her smile revealed big perfect teeth. Her no nonsense long, dark and wavy hair matched her what-you-see-is-what-you-get apparel, a look many women pay tons of money to imitate.

When I removed the last chair from the truck, a gnarly brown spider scurried toward my foot and its demise. I tossed the chair from inside the cab and heard Susannah yelp and the chair crash to the ground. I ignored both and began my ritualistic war cries and killing of the spider. When it was over, somehow I knew that Susannah would

be behind me. She was. It didn't look like the
flying chair had hit her. She said nothing. I offered
nothing. We finished setting up the house.

A month later we had the certificate of
occupancy for a new house. Once again, Susannah
and I were the sum total of the moving crew. We
had barely started unloading when Susannah
screamed from the back of the house. I ran toward
her distressed voice. I found her pressed in a corner
of the kitchen. Not five feet away a green snake
uncoiled itself. Surely the snake grew equally
frightened and perturbed by her screeching as she
was of its presence.

I moved in and snatched up the snake. I
took it outside and deposited it in the woods behind
the house. I came back in, expecting a hero's
welcome.

"How is it that you're petrified of spiders,
but you have no reservations handling a snake?"
Susannah asked.

"I used to be a member of a primitive
Southern Baptist church," I said.

She chuckled, but my humor didn't get me
off the hook.

"Really, you lost it with the itsy bitsy spider.
With the snake you were calm, and I've never seen
anything as careful and gentle as when you put it
out in the yard."

"I just don't like spiders."

"Don't like them. You stomped that little
guy ten times after it was long dead. Do you have
arachnophobia?" she asked.

"I'm not afraid of spiders. I kill them," I
told her.

"Uh huh. Whatever. I saw you turn into a schoolgirl that time a spider was in the moving truck."

"School girls hide in corners and scream. I'm not afraid of anything. I kill spiders."

"I wasn't hiding and you did some hollering and yelling of your own while attacking the spider. Tell you what, let's call it even," she said. We smiled and endured an uncomfortable moment of not knowing if we should shake hands, hug or what. I sort of wanted to hug.

"That'll work," I agreed.

"I'm glad you set the snake free. Killing things is just plain bad karma. You ought to be careful. You may come back in the next life as a spider," she warned.

"You're welcome," I said, wanting to change the subject. It dawned on me that I had no need to wait until the next life; I already was a spider. My previous revelation was that as much as I destroyed each and every spider, I killed off a little piece of that disgusting house and my own mama. In that instant I saw that karma had already taken affect. I killed a part of myself, that which I hate, with every spider. It never got any better because like the first spider, the one that escaped on that stormy morning, there's something inside of me that I can't find to eliminate.

"It can be very dangerous not to fear anything," Susannah said, breaking my deep thought. "I learned that from the guys. Once you meet them you'll see what I mean."

As Susannah spoke I took note that I was afraid. I feared myself. I had no idea what I would be capable of and what I might do if I ever really exploded. She made me think. I liked that as much

as I was coming to like her.  It was a shame
Susannah was more than five years older than me.

"Okay, I lied.  I do have fears.  I'm terribly
afraid of rejection.  Can I buy you dinner when we
finish here?"

## Chapter 48

"Why would she say that, any of it? Hasn't she done enough to me already? I didn't need to know all that about Duke's daddy, and I sure as hell didn't want to hear how my father had raped her. Does she hate me that much?"

"Maybe she loves you that much to confide in you. She trusts you that much to be vulnerable. Perhaps she knows you love her that much to listen. Her whole life was a cancer eating away at her. She knew you could hear her story, you could understand it. You could help her shoulder the burden. She respected you enough to be strong for her and strong for yourself and break the cycle of despair. She had hope. Hope for you and hope in you."

"Or she was plain old evil," I suggested. The thought came to me as I looked at an icon of the crucifixion on the wall behind Father Petrie. I thought it odd that the artist captured such a loving act so gruesomely.

"You don't believe that," Father Petrie said.

"Do you believe all that hogwash about love, trust and hope?"

"Yes and no," he said. "Those are things healthy families do. Given what I know about you and your mother, you two aren't the type to openly say 'I love you' or 'I'm feeling exposed.' Instead you did and said what you had to in order to get your needs met. Your hostile manner of interacting took the form of normalcy for you."

"I can see the theory, but it gets lost in perception. My mother couldn't bear to live with Duke. The whole time I thought he was always trying to come back home. As it turns out, he wanted to stay away. Back then I spent a lot of time and energy acting out, hoping to get sent to a home with him. All the while he was threatening mama's life if she sent me away like she did to him."

"You're correct. Reality and perception come together differently. If I had taught in the seminary instead of taking a parish I would have written a book. I've found that olfactory, visual, and auditory senses send chemicals to your brain and that dictates your disposition and vernacular."

"Say what?" I asked.

"I'm suggesting that your senses tell you how to act in a given setting. Do you follow?"

"It's not crystal clear to me, but keep on and I'll let you know if I get lost," I said.

"Forget about the book idea for a minute. The way I understand it, your mother acted in a way that made sense for the both of you. Think about it. If she had asked you to hear her heartache there's little chance you would have accepted. She had no choice but to force it on you. That's the way you do. You couldn't refuse her then."

I liked talking with Father Petrie. Dr. Hayes was straightforward, but Petrie seemed less reserved and even more direct. His questions made me think, not hurt. His office was even different. His work space was filled with trinkets, keepsakes, books and more crosses than I'd ever seen. The room felt inviting, not institutional.

"Maybe you should write that book. I just had a revelation. The last time I saw my brother he was in prison. It was a harsh visit. It started out awkward. I expected that, but it spiraled into ugliness. We cussed and shouted at each other, a very normal thing for us to do. As I think about your theory and look back on that last visit I can see how we were just two stupid guys trying to be hard and to care of each other at the same time. In the end we made some tough choices that we have lived with ever since."

"What happened?" Father Petrie asked.

"We parted ways, indefinitely."

"Do you miss him?" he asked.

"Of course. I've spent my whole life missing him. That's what I do," I said.

"Did you find a way to let him know that?"

"Yeah. You won't believe this, but I simply told him."

"Let me guess. He reacted poorly."

"Man, are you good! As I recall this is the second time you deserved to win a prize for the correct answer," I said. "Yeah, Duke got all hostile and told me that we are gas and fire."

"He only wants the best for you." I knew the pastor was right. I don't know why, but I didn't tell him about my lip reading of Duke's final words to me."

"It's the same with your mother. She played a dangerous game with anger and guilt."

"That's a harder pill to swallow," I said.

"Steve, you have a good heart, but you, too, have engaged in a dangerous game with guilt and anger. The time has come for you to trade those in for inner peace and love. Have you ever really loved anyone?" Father Petrie asked.

"Now see, that's a bunch of minister talk you're giving me," I said.

"So it is. Can you answer my question?"

## Chapter 49

"I noticed you almost involuntarily go back and forth between slang and a noticeably educated vocabulary," Dr. Hayes said after I gave her a then and now comparison of my situation. She had asked me about my future plans. She advocated for college. I let her know I was thinking that, too, just not right now.

"There are many faces of me, one from the group home, one from the neighborhood, one I use with Duke, another for the Carpenters, and an entirely different one for you and school."

"We all have faces and masks we put on in certain situations. I'm curious as to your constantly improving vocabulary and articulation."

"I don't have a secret. I read books. Reading kept me out of the common area in the group home and out of trouble since then," I said.

"You haven't mentioned your appreciation of reading previously," she said.

"I'm not like a geek or anything. I don't read in the lunchroom or for pleasure."

"If you know the benefits of reading, why do it secretly?" Dr. Hayes asked.

"It's not like I'm afraid to be seen with a book. I don't close the door to trouble. I always stand my ground. That's how I built the rep that protects me."

"Rep, as in reputation?" Dr. Hayes clarified.

"Yes."

"And, what is your reputation?" she asked.

"I'll fight. I come fair, but if you want to mix it up, I can go to legs. Back in the group home there was no other option. Day in and day out we'd fight, sometimes several times before lunch. No matter what happened, it was never enough. Somebody always had something to prove something or was mad and wanted to go a round or two. Win or lose, somebody else stood ready and stepped up to take the next shot."

"Is that all you are, a fighter?" asked Dr. Hayes.

"It has worked for me in every place I land. I was born into it and it keeps me from being something else," I said.

"There's something worse than being a fighter. Is that what I'm hearing you say?" she asked.

I folded my arms across my chest and nodded. She scribbled on her pad. I had come today with a new agenda. I knew I had to put my best stuff out to her. I breathed deeply, dropped my arms to my sides and made a conscious effort not to play the role of shoe gazer, not today.

"Yes, but I don't want to talk about it right now. Maybe before I leave."

Dr. Hayes was still writing as she asked, "Okay, what do you read?"

"Whatever I get assigned in school." I said.

"Do you have a favorite book?"

"I read *The World According to Garp*. I liked it. It took a while. I got mad at the story a lot, but I liked it over all when I finally finished it," I told her.

"Why did the book upset you?"

"I didn't like when things kept going so badly for Garp. It made me close my eyes. I don't like thinking about it. It's the same with dying." I said. Dr. Hayes looked puzzled. I continued, "When death comes to mind I have to clear my head. I don't like thinking about it."

"Does this happen any other times or with other books?" she asked.

"The only other time I can recall is when I saw a movie, *The Breakfast Club*."

"I know that movie. What part caused you to need to cleanse your head?" Dr. Hayes asked.

"When the guy Judd Nelson played caved to the principal who got up in his face," I said.

"Yes, okay, I remember that part." I could almost see the thoughts swimming around her head. She looked up at me and said, "You've told me that you know pain. Why does seeing someone struggle in a movie or reading about it upset you so?"

"Isn't that a question I should be asking you?" I asked honestly.

"Can you answer the question?"

"That's how I feel. How I react. I'm not sure that I know why," I confessed.

Dr. Hayes jotted a note and said, "Thinking about the movie, I can see you in a couple of the characters, but you're most like the Judd Nelson character. What would you have done if you were in his place?"

"If anybody, even a principal, came up on me like that we would go a round. I ain't saying I can take a grown man, but you can bet your life I would have gotten in a few licks and taken some skin. I believe you have to make the other guy feel it. So he knows he's been in a fight. My buddy MD got cut up something awful in a fight when we were kids. I remember being in the hospital waiting room thinking if it had been me I'd rather die than live with a loss. Ol' Judd Nelson should of done the same," I said harshly.

"Do you have any idea what causes you to fight? Is it pride, ego, your 'rep' or what is it?" she asked.

"It's all I can do. Nothing else eases the aching."

"What hurts you?" she asked, as her fine point pencil rapidly glided across the pad noting God knows what.

"In the time I've been coming to see you I have learned a lot. It bugs me to no end, but I have seen my mistakes and shortcomings. I'm man enough to admit that you're right. When I think about this whole mess I have named a ton of scapegoats. I blamed my mom, the house, the authorities, the Carpenters and at times I've even blamed you for my pain. My nature and nurture battle is one of existence. How I came into existence and how I'll make a life of it. The great tragedy of life is I was born to live to die."

"I see you read Nietzsche in school."

"I have," I said proudly.

"I'm sorry I interrupted. Please keep going," Dr. Hayes instructed.

"I figure Nietzsche would see my cultural constructs are just as tragic. The world I was raised in and keep landing in is cruel and violent. My little part is only a fraction of the wraithlike world around me. I never seem to take up residence in a world of peace and happiness. That hurts worse than living in a nasty house and being poor. At least then I knew myself and my world view was not greater than my reality. My life is a bad book or a movie. I have this tension between angels and demons. I live with all my demons and that's okay. I need an angel, just one to come and help me defeat the evil inside of me."

"I'm impressed," Dr. Hayes said. "However, that sounded well-rehearsed. You have been mindful of our process. This is a big step to take ownership and to have a clear concept of what you want from life."

"I couldn't have made these decisions a year ago. I'm well aware that broader means and noble influences have made their way to me of late. I've bathed in them. Yet I'm far from cleansed on the inside. You, the Carpenters, Julie, Natalie…you've all been agents of change. But it's time I take the reins. If I can't fix this from the inside out, then what's point? I've got to do this."

"I'm not sure what it is you feel you have to do," she said.

"I'm of age now. There are no charges pending against me. I'm going to move out of the Carpenters' house and I'm going to stop coming to see you. I'm done. It's time to man up and to take care of my own house," I stated.

"Surely you understand that your treatment is much more than that. You've made a small breakthrough here, but you have been through enormous tragedy and your social response mechanisms are immature and barbaric. You are not ready to go it alone. You can get hurt, hurt yourself, and certainly undo all the work we have completed together."

"Let me tell you a story," I said. "An old tire hung from a two inch thick rope strung around a tree limb. The homemade swing dangled over one of the deepest parts of the creek. My brother said it had been there since anyone could remember. He showed the swing to me when I was about ten. As was his custom, Duke shamed me on to the hanging contraption and then pushed me out over the water.

Unlike your standard thrill ride, I had no inherent sense of safety. I knew my brother's callous sense of amusement wouldn't let me stop. I knew trying to jump to the other side would result in rocks, limbs and God knows what else jabbing into my feet or body. Falling in the middle of the water seemed foreboding as I was anything but a strong swimmer. All that would get me was cold, wet and shame at best and possibly drowned. I settled for that, though, as jumping to the other side and running away meant being an even bigger sissy.

"Sometime later I took my friends to the tire swing and that made a hero of me for the day. By then the banks had eased back due to erosion. Now it was a trick just to get on the swing. You had to run, leap and actually grab hold of the swing midair. Like before, to get off the swing the options were to drop in the water or jump from the swing and hope for a soft landing on the bank without taking a limb to the chest. The latter was much easier said than done. Most often we flopped into the chilly waters," I said, focusing my eyes. Just talking about it took me back. I could see, feel and smell everything just the way it used to be.

"Steve, albeit that was a nice story, it has no bearing on the serious decision you are trying to make unilaterally," she said showing her concern. All of a sudden I knew she cared. My case was not about a write up in a professional journal or professional curiosity. She cared. That helped. Unfortunately, one way or another, caring relationships never worked out for me.

"Here are the two ways my trip down memory lane is relevant. First, even to this day, the creek is the only thing I know to be true. Second, on that day I learned about a beautiful thing in an ugly way. Later on when I shared it with my friends, I didn't mention my initial fear or humiliation. All I did was share the goodness. And if only for a day, I did a good thing. So, I have determined through my time with you that there must be a way to use the ugliness in my life to bring about something good the same as you do by seeing people like me. It has to help or else you wouldn't put yourself through misery every day. I intend to figure out how I can do just the same," I said.

"You have no idea why I do this, more importantly, you know it's not that simple. Your life, your anger, your healing, it's all very complicated," Dr. Hayes warned.

"I did everything you asked me. I told you the truth. At first, I came because I had no choice. I cooperated because you're pretty and I liked talking to you. Then I grew to respect you and the process. As the process began to make sense to me I tried to guess what you'd ask or say next. I got pretty good at that, too. I tried to think of what you wrote on your pad. I wanted to get better. I changed all right, but I'm not better."

"You are only thinking about one aspect of this multifaceted situation," she cautioned.

"You may be right. You taught me to consider consequences. I learned that it's too much trouble to battle with my conscience. Without one, I can be like a force of nature. I can be a powerful hurricane accountable only to my gale. Not moral, but terrible and beautiful."

"What is it you hope to achieve?" Dr. Hayes asked in a voice that sounded surprisingly unsympathetic.

"Meaning. Wholeness. Belonging. If there are such things."

"They do exist and you can bask in them, but you need time and assistance."

"I'm tired of people helping. The way I see it, you opened a wound and left it gaping and oozing for me to attend. I plan to do just that."

"I hear you and I want to help you," Dr. Hayes said, almost desperately.

"Tell you what," I said. "I'll give you my journal and take yet another one. I give you my word that I'll keep writing and sending the journals to you. Other than that, I'm finished with words. Thanks for all you've done for me." I moved to get up and leave.

"Don't do this. We have a lot of work to do. Your walking out now is like leaving mid-sentence," Dr. Hayes said as I walked toward the door.

"Say a prayer for me if you are inclined to do that sort of thing."

## Chapter 50

I intentionally played Bruce Springsteen's *Independence Day* as I put away a few little grocery items I had purchased. Afterwards, I unpacked the last of my boxes. It didn't take long, as I didn't own too much. I felt like such a grown up. I decided to embrace the moment and look around at my space. It was the first place that I could call my own...my very own. I rewound the cassette tape to play *Independence Day* again. I took a turn about the room.

When I had answered the classified ad for an efficiency, I hadn't known that was the equivalent of a one room apartment. The place came furnished. At first, I felt a little weird and grossed out by using other people's furnishings, but I told myself it was no different than hotel rooms. But then again, I hadn't been in too many of them. I finished my self-guided tour of the efficiency before the first chorus of the song. I thought about the song. It was scary, liberating, and tentative all at once. I felt the same way. I decided to go ahead and make dinner.

I grabbed a can of chili and dropped it, hard, on the counter. I realized without looking that I didn't own a can opener. Hoorah for independence! I decided to go for the old faithful peanut butter and jelly sandwich. As I returned the can of chili to the cabinet, I saw that I had no peanut butter, either. Everybody had peanut butter. Even mama always had peanut butter. I plopped down on the floor and leaned against the kitchenette cabinets and sang along as the tape continued to play into the room. I decided to pass on dinner, and gave my new place a finger-blistering cleaning.

As I dusted, polished and scrubbed I replayed a recent conversation with the Carpenters in my head.

"You don't have to go," Mrs. Carpenter said.

"I know. I feel like I should have my own space, though," I told her.

"Have we done something to upset you?" Mrs. Carpenter asked.

"Y'all have been nothing but good to me. I have to do this for me."

Always the pragmatic one, Dr. Carpenter wanted to know, "Where will you go?"

"I'm going to rent a place in town."

"How can we help?" Mrs. Carpenter asked.

"I'm all set. I've paid the deposits and everything."

"When can we see it?" she asked.

"As soon as I get unpacked, I'll have y'all over for dinner." Remembering that statement caused me to suspend work momentarily. I emptied the mop bucket and thought about how I needed to make a thorough list before my next trip to the market. I couldn't even feed myself at this point. I grabbed a pen. The only pad I had was my journal. I figured it would be okay to use a page for a grocery list. As I jotted down items, I thought back to the conversation.

"What about college?" Mrs. Carpenter asked.

"That's part of what I'm doing. I'm trying to make a plan and not just go through the motions. I'm not ready for college. I think it'll be good for me to work for a while and figure out what I want to do. I promise I won't be trying to find myself for

twenty years." That got a smile from them both. I
was aiming, however, for an all out chuckle.

"We love you. You know that," Dr.
Carpenter said.

"I'm just moving. I've lost enough in my
life. I want to do this for me, but I don't want to
lose you. I can never repay you for what you've
done for me."

"You don't have to…"

"I know that. I do. I know we are family."

## Chapter 51

"I appreciate you keeping me hooked up after everything that's happened," I said to my old friend.

"We're brothers, man. Where you live don't matter to me," Bubba said as we gave a strong embrace and banged each other on the back. I had talked to him several times on the phone. This was the first time I had laid eyes on my childhood friend in years. My, how he had grown! When puberty struck I had the first growth spurt. I enjoyed a short term as the biggest guy in our neighborhood. Bubba had caught up and kept going. He stood tall and solid as an ox.

"Damn. Are you on steroids?" I asked jokingly.

"I was wondering if your NT ass stopped eating."

"NT. I haven't heard that in years," I said.

"I guess you haven't been hearing Fat Boy too much these days. I like the skinny look on you, Fat Boy."

"For real. It's good to see you. I know I'm not all that popular with people from the past."

"Man, we've been through too much. Besides, the only room they kept clean in my house was the kitchen and that was so the old man could cook and cut up crack."

"Stop it," I said uncomfortably.

"You know it's for real. And it ain't just us. All the houses I've broken into. Everybody's got some trouble or something they don't want seen by all the good folks. You know what I mean?"

"Do I ever," I admitted. We had met at Ray Ray's. It was a decrepit double-wide trailer that sat

at the entrance of a trailer park. Ray-Ray managed
to keep the doors of his nasty little joint open by
serving minors. Bubba gripped his can of Bud. I
had a Coke. We both pulled a chug and then set our
cans on the shabby felt of the pool table. We
flipped a coin to decide who would bust the rack.
He won.

"Your brother made parole," Bubba said
before sinking two stripes on the break. He was an
ace. I knew this game would soon be over and I'd
be out ten bucks.

"How do you know?" I asked.

"It pays to know things. Oh yeah, I'm sorry
to hear about your old lady. She was always good
to me," Bubba said and clinched his lips.

"Thanks. What do I owe you?"

"For the information, nothing. Not yet
anyway. Your boy Duke disappeared into the
woodwork."

"What do you mean?"

"He drew his walking papers and strolled,"
Bubba said as he straddled the table and made
another unbelievable shot. The floor of the old
trailer creaked as he walked around the table,
eyeing the balls in play.

"What about his parole officer?"

"He's due to check in next week," Bubba
said.

"You'll let me know what happens, right?"

Bubba dropped the twelve ball and called
for the eight in the side pocket.

"If I call you, stop by the bank before you
come my way." The eight ball drifted in the hole
with ease. "For now I hope you've got a ten on
you."

"Say, man while you're pummeling me here, why don't you give me an update on the crew?"

"You're probably the only one that cares about that lot of heathens," Bubba said.

"You said it. We're brothers," I said.

"Brothers. So we are. Here's what's up with our brothers. MD's dad and that hag finally parted ways. MD went with his dad. I hear they're living in Alabama trying to make a living selling junk at trading days and flea markets. You know Caddie's uncle works on cars in his carport.

"Uh huh."

"Well, Caddie helps out when there's extra work. Other than that he drinks for a living if you know what I mean."

I nodded. Bubba continued his masterful game while bringing me up to date on our old running buddies.

"Silo's getting by. He's still trying to find a get rich scheme that doesn't require him to do anything except to count money. Here's the heartbreaker. Our boy Paul, he's not so bold anymore. He got pulled over and acted all tough. This time all his lip got him shot. He didn't do much time over it, but he's paralyzed on the left side of his body. He lives in a little hospital for the handicapped. I saw him once or twice. It's fucked up. You won't like what you see, but you ought to go visit him."

"I reckon I should. Dare I ask what you are doing?"

"This is it. I play well, exchange info and get paid."

"I break next. I never even got a shot. You need to join the pro circuit."

Bubba flashed a smile and repeated, "Like I said, I'm getting paid," and he snapped the ten dollar bill from my fingers.

"What's up with the old neighborhood?" I asked and chalked my unused cue stick. "I about lost my mind when I saw all the big houses over there."

"Man, that shit's fucked up, isn't it? I rode through there and for nothing but to see old Stefi. I knocked on her window and some little fag started screaming. His gayfer boyfriend ran out wearing boxer shorts with flowers on them. The little queenie came out toting a golf club. Both the little bitches were prissing around, talking about calling the cops. You know I had to spilt that scene, and with no Stefi. Man, that's the part that freakin' sucked."

"I thought y'all had long been over," I said.

"Stefi was always good for a romp. That girl could bo-hawg," he said gritting his teeth and grinning through them.

"Bo-hawg? What in the world are you talking about?"

"You know that girl could get down and do it hard," Bubba said while bending his knees, gripping his fists, raising his arms and dropping them like he was trying to break a two by four over his knee.

"She was a wild ride. I guess bo-hawg sums it up," I agreed.

"You didn't have to remind me you did her, too," said Bubba, in a tone somewhere between humor and anger.

"Whatever," I said jokily.

"Are we going to play pool or not?" Bubba asked.

I smashed the pyramid of ceramic balls. The black eight ball sailed into the upper left hand corner pocket. I peeled off another ten and handed it to Bubba.

He flashed his winning smile again and announced, "Some things never change."

I thought to myself that some things do nothing but change.

## Chapter 52

Gloria and Father Petrie convinced a local paint store to donate gallons of interior and exterior paint for the houses. The store even gave away good colors, not just the stuff they couldn't sell. Susannah and I scheduled work days at each of the houses over a period of a couple of months. We brought the paint, food, iced tea and lemonade. Along with the men who lived in each house, we painted inside and out.

When we met to spruce up the house where I worked, a couple of the fellows, Doc and Leon, made a major fuss over Susannah. The two guys attended to her like queen's servants. Dressed in camouflage pants, a faded sweatshirt and a bandana wrapped around her head to cover her hair, Susannah looked more practical than pretty. That was her style. Showing just that, she promptly placed paintbrushes in both of their hands and put the guys to work.

Susannah had brought a boom box. All morning long it blared out the sultry lyrics and melodies of 10,000 Maniacs. She sang, swayed and painted with the music. She was a vision to behold. I found I wasn't the only one watching.

"Youngblood, that there is a fine woman. She's got it all. You need to get with dat and hang tight," Doc said. He, Leon and I stood watching as she worked circles around us. Doc had been with the program since day one. He wanted very badly to return to his former life. He had a family and he had worked as a paramedic.

Leon was another story. He talked a good game, but he rarely made any effort to make a change in his life. Today was no different. He spent most of his time eating and talking while we all scraped, taped and painted.

At the end of the day, Susannah and I took the water hose and rinsed out the brushes and rollers while the guys finished up the sandwiches and polished of the drinks. We folded the drop cloths. Preparing for and cleaning up afterwards seemed more like drudgery than the actual painting.

"Do they all call you Youngblood?" she asked as we carried the drop cloths to the car.

"Yeah. I don't know if they even know my name. They've called me Youngblood since the beginning."

"You have a great rapport with the guys. I had worried about you being so young. You really connect with them. That's a gift."

Susannah had no idea. Not one of us would agree that the many levels on which the guys and I connected were a gift. Right then a car pulled up and scored some dope. Susannah and I watched and said nothing.

"You know the fellows are one thing, but all of our houses are surrounded by trouble. Do you have something to protect yourself?" I asked.

"I have pepper spray in my bag."

"Do you ever think about having something a little more intimidating? When I was a kid we took pepper spray and mace in the face for sport."

"You were a messed up kid," she said, laughingly.

"You have no idea."

"These little drug dealers don't worry me. They're just trying to make money. They don't want to draw unnecessary attention to themselves," Susannah said, indicating the crack house across the street.

"I guess you're right," I said. I decided not to go any further. I didn't want to admit I carried a gun or to have to lie about it. I changed the subject.

"I had a great time working with you today. I was afraid it might be awkward."

"Why, because you're completely smitten with me?" she said with a penetrating smile.

"No, because I caught you looking at my butt when I was unloading the car," I said.

"I wasn't the only one."

"Okay, so I did sneak a peek at your behind when you were up on the ladder taping the window sills," I said.

"Oh, I know that. I meant that I wasn't the only one looking at you."

"Stop it!" I said. Wow. I had a great day of working, of belonging and of loving. I didn't get a chance to bask in the moment.

"You never talk about your family," Susannah said. "Are your parents still living?"

I hemmed and hawed before finally answering. "My family life is complicated."

"I think all families are complicated. I hope I didn't bring up a sore subject," Susannah said. I loved her response. I had met her mother and Susannah had always been respectful of my space. She made me comfortable enough to at least talk about my family.

"I was adopted. My adopted parents are very much alive and well."

"Do they live nearby? I'd love to meet them sometime."

Instantly I drifted back in time to my dear sweet childhood girlfriend, Rhonda. Must all the good ones ask to see inside the fence? I remember breaking up with Rhonda over the same question.

Like everything in the world around me I had
changed.  My family had changed.  This time I had
something presentable.  I thought about it.  On this
very day, I was trying to follow my beloved
Rhonda's admonition to do noble things.  I
wondered where life had led Rhonda.  I decided that
wherever she was, she'd want me to make a good
choice.  So I did.

   Since we had been dating I had met
Susannah's mother.  I knew the request she made
was fair.  She had never brought up my family
before today.  Her words and demeanor had always
been respectful of me and my space.  I acquiesced.
"I have an idea.  I'll cook dinner and you can come
and meet them," I said.

   "That sounds wonderful.  Let's plan it."

# Reckoning
## Chapter 53

Salad, baked potatoes and steak made up the menu of my first ever dinner party. I planned a meal hard to foul up and easy to please. I invited the Carpenters and Susannah. I set out to kill the proverbial two birds with one stone. Having them over for a meal would make Mrs. Carpenter exceedingly happy. Introducing my adopted parents to Susannah would please her at the same time.

The idea of actually inviting people into my living space felt like spiders crawling on my skin. I cleaned my apartment and then cleaned it again. I burned incense I had bought at a Christian bookstore to make the place smell like church. I decided against playing background music. I knew the Carpenters didn't like anything from my limited collection. I beamed as I set out my matching plates and silverware. I had purchased the setting for four at a flea market. I didn't know what I'd do if I ever needed to feed five people.

The Carpenters arrived early. That was their way. Just then I noticed I didn't have four chairs around the dinner table. I didn't even have a grand total of four chairs in the apartment. Dr. Carpenter happily went back out and picked up some folding chairs for me. Mrs. Carpenter stayed at the apartment with me to greet Susannah. Everything worked out. Dr. Carpenter made it back in time and we set out the chairs. Moments later Susannah entered my humble domain, looking radiant.

Like the guys at the house, the Carpenters flocked to Susannah and her charms. They went even further, as she appealed to their intellect and sensibilities. Susannah glided through conversations on her background, education, the declining interest among freshmen in liberal arts, increasing mortgage rates and her thoughts on running for elected office in the future. I had no idea about the latter before tonight. In the end, I think I might have been the happiest of all with my little get together.

## Chapter 54

"I heard my brother got released from prison. The best I can tell is he went nomad. I checked with all his buddies and his old hang outs. There's no sign of him. He vanished. He could be like any one of the guys I work with at the house. For that matter, I could be like any one of those guys. I guess that's why I do it, besides the fact that work keeps my mind off of life."

"Be careful, people have a tendency to create what they fear," Father Petrie said.

"I don't fear homelessness," I said, defensively.

"What do you fear?" the pastor asked.

"Myself," I paused and finished. "I'm afraid of me." Father Petrie gave a look of understanding. No, it was more like a look of confirmation of something he already knew. He swiveled his chair around and sifted through the clutter on his credenza.

He spun back to face me and trusted a tattered paperback toward me.

"Here, let me give you a book. It's about Saint Francis of Assisi."

"Why are you giving this to me?" I asked Father Petrie, without taking hold of the book.

"I know you probably didn't learn or talk about saints much in your old church."

"Yeah, but why are you giving me a book?" I repeated.

"I want you to read it so we can…" I lost track of what he was saying. I felt something awful welling up in me. It came out and I interrupted.

"I'm sorry, but I'm not a good keeper of books," I said curtly.

"Don't be silly. It's an old paper back. What harm can come from you reading it?" Father Petrie asked.

"My mama gave me a book once. I was in grade school and had recently discovered reading. It was a gift for my birthday when mama gave me the book. It was the kind with pop up pictures. I had a hissy fit. I was a boy. I didn't want a book. I wanted a G.I. Joe. I took that book and cut it up into a million little pieces," I said emotionally.

"I know you read. You've talked about it before," he said.

"Yes, I've come to enjoy reading, but that was the last time someone gave me a book. I haven't thought about that in forever."

"This is my only copy," he said, shaking the book in his right hand. "Don't cut it, even into large pieces." We both laughed. "Do you want to talk about the book your mom gave you?" he asked gently.

"Not really. I know she didn't have much money. I know she wanted to encourage me to read and that's about the best thing a parent can do for a child. I know I knew better then. That's why I'm finished with talking about the subject."

"That's fine. Seems like you've got the big picture. You don't have to take the book to be polite." He drew it back and placed it on his desk. Every day I grew to like this guy more. He affirmed me and he let me move slowly, but he made sure I moved. I picked up the book and examined it.

"Isn't Saint Francis an animal lover or something?" I asked.

"He's much more than that," Father Petrie instructed. "Francis was the first person to make a connection between all of nature as a part of worship, prayer and a means of relating to God."

"I like that," I said, and I let the concept take hold in my mind.

"I thought you would, hence I'm 'loaning' you the book." We both smiled at his overemphasis on the word *loaning*. He really understood me. That meant the world to me. I pulled the book closer and thumbed through the pages. Father Petrie kept talking as I glanced at the dog eared and highlighted pages.

"There's more, much more. Francis was a monk. He rejected the world and was rejected by the world. But here's the other part that made me think of you. Francis came to God as a sinner. He understood his wretchedness and brokenness and that allowed him to serve the Lord."

"You're very thoughtful and considerate," I said gratefully.

"It's part of my job."

"You're good at it."

"I think you could be, too. There's a place for you in the church," Father Petrie said confidently.

I closed the worn book and looked up at Father Petrie while his last words still hung in the air.

"Whoa there, Padre! One step at a time. I'll read the book.

## Chapter 55

Dear Dr. Hayes:

I hope you are doing well. Things are going okay for me. As I promised, I am sending you my journal. You'll be glad to know that after all this time I have finally come to appreciate journaling. This was the first one where I read back through the pages. I found there is a great deal to learn from recognizing that I'm making the same old mistakes and also for being able to clearly see when and where I climb out of a hole. Shame on me for not noticing sooner.

You probably know that I moved out of the Carpenters' house. There's a page or two about that in the journal. It's been a difficult transition, much more than I anticipated. I got knocked down by a couple of little things I never saw coming. Picking myself up has helped me to be careful and pay closer attention to details.

I have been in the same relationship with a woman for some time now. Her name is Susannah. I try to be open and honest with her (not about everything of course--she's not ready for that. I'm not ready for that). I did introduce her to the Carpenters. How about that? Anyway, I do my best to treat her with respect. We both work for the same organization. I hardly ever see her at work. I have learned a lot from her about helping others and about how to be a good friend.

I know you had concerns about the church I attend. I'm still worshipping there. It's proven to be a good place for me. I feel connected to the world again. I've made friends. It was a church member who offered me a job. I have been talking with the pastor there. He's an interesting character.

The whole experience is drawing me closer to the belonging and meaning that I told you I hoped to find.

Don't worry about sending a new journal to me. I already bought one. I know that I have responsibilities in my own healing process. I will keep sending the journals to you until you say for me to stop. That's not a hint for you to do that. There's a lot more going on with me, but I have mentioned all the important stuff in the journal. I made sure not to hold out on you.

All the best,

Steve

## Chapter 56

"Of course the starter went out on my car. I was pissed. Oops! I'm sorry," I apologized.

"I'm not offended. You know me well enough by now," Father Petrie said. "Go on with your story."

"I had to ride the bus. That took forever. I ran the last couple of blocks. I checked in with an elderly lady at the information desk and found out I couldn't see her for a while. I stepped into the restroom and splashed water on my face and neck to cool down. Once I cleaned up I bought a Coke and went into the waiting room.

All the worn out seats were full of people with long faces. I stood propped against the door trying to breathe normally. It didn't help. Sweat beaded all over me. My shirt clung to my chest and back. I felt the eyes of her family heavy on me. Tension took up more space in the little antiseptic room than the cheap furnishings. No one said a word. Not even a hello, I'm glad you are here. Nothing. I went to hug her mother. She stepped back and let me know she used to think a lot of me, but now I had fallen from her grace."

"Give her time. This kind of thing is hard on everyone," Father Petrie said.

"I can't decide what's worse, what happened or being made out as the bad guy. It's not like I'm a stranger to the role, but I didn't do anything wrong here."

"Trust me, they will all come around once the shock wears off and nothing will be more important than your presence. It'll all be okay," the pastor assured me.

"They may calm down, but I get the sense it will never be okay, not with me. Dr. Hayes, the group home counselors, the Carpenters and just about every person who knows the truth about my situation told me that the worst was over and I could get on with my life. They all said there's a world of opportunity out there for me, but between reliving the past in therapy and the chaos of life in the present my condition keeps degenerating into a raging hell of disparity."

I had met Father Petrie in a donut shop. As I stirred large amounts of cream and sugar into my coffee I felt exposed. It dawned on me that we were out in the open talking about very personal stuff rather than in the privacy of his eccentric office. Dr. Hayes had never offered me coffee and a pastry, but her swanky office gave way to privacy to a fault. Father Petrie actually dunked his donut. Milk, maybe, but black coffee, yuk!

"You should try it. You'll like it," he said, and took a bite of the soggy donut.

"I'm not hungry. All I can think about is how it's my fault Susannah had a miscarriage. Nothing good ever came from my mama. Nothing good will ever come from me, especially not a precious little baby."

"You can't blame yourself. Miscarriages involve a variety of physical and biological things that contribute to them and you are not one," Father Petrie said.

"Oh, but I can blame myself. This is the second year in a row that a girl was pregnant during the month of my birthday. The first one told me about it and promptly had an abortion with no input whatsoever from me. I was wrecked. My mama's stuff was as messy as can be and she never gave up on a baby.  I don't know for sure when the baby becomes a real life.  But I feel like that girl killed something innocent.  She murdered part of me, the only innocent part of me.  Now, Susannah had a miscarriage.  I can't take this.  I'm numb.  God damn, enough already.  I need to know how this happened.  I've learned to trace consequences to the root and I didn't do anything.  I'm not to blame.  This one's on God.  God chose this, not me."

"God doesn't single out people.  I'm sorry, too, but there is no simple answer.  The world is complex and God..."

I lost concern for my public surroundings and interrupted, "I don't think you fucking understand.  I need an answer!"

"I can't give you an answer.  Not one that will have meaning."

"Who can?" I demanded.

"Don't think this is a pat answer, but you are going to have to take your concerns up with God.  Be as mad as you like.  I feel certain God can take it.  There's a lot of good that can come from protest theology."

"From what?"

"That's where you bring your anger to the feet of God.  You blame God.  You let God know how angry, confused and hurt you are by actions you don't understand."

"I'm not sure that makes sense to me.  I understand God punishing the wicked.  I can live with bad things happening to sinners like me, but Susannah, she didn't do anything.  And the baby. What did it ever do?  God can punish me.  I'll man up and take it, but Jesus, why did this have to happen to them?  Do I have to spend my whole life in solitary like back in the group home?"

"You and Susannah both do important work in the name of the Lord. God has a reason for all that happens and I know God has plans for you and Susannah. Being together or having children may be a part of that in the future, just not now," Father Petrie counseled.

"Before, you asked me if I ever loved anyone. I tried to love Susannah. This morning she called and told me not to come back to the hospital. She said not to come at all. That's cool.

"Up until now, she always treated me well and I tried to do the same. I tried to be thoughtful with her and show her respect. I don't know if that's love. What I do know is pain. I got hit by a car when I got mad at my fifth grade teacher and walked home. I took buckshot in the back of the leg when a guy caught me caught stealing boat motors. I was stabbed in the chest in the group home, for no good reason at all. I lived in a house knee high with trash. I'm telling you I know pain. Losing this baby that I've never seen, never will see, hurts worse than anything I've ever felt. I loved it. I don't even know if it was a boy or a girl, but I love it."

## Chapter 57

"Fifty feet of moss and algae-covered rocks beneath a downspout of the creek made for a grand waterslide. We called that part of the creek, Slippery Rocks. This was our version of a Slip-N-Slide. It's amusing that all we thought of was the fun we had splashing and sliding the muggy summer days away, but every walk home from Slippery Rocks managed to draw our attention to the vast scrapes and scratches incurred by the rocks, pebbles and sand. We were poor, but not stupid. After a couple of painful trips wobbling back to the neighborhood, we got smart and left old blue jeans at the top of Slippery Rocks. Even the denim couldn't protect our legs and behinds from the damage. In the end, the zipping and slipping in the cool waters of the creek always seemed worth the minor discomfort," I said, recalling it like it was yesterday.

"You light up like a Christmas tree every time you talk about this creek of yours," Father Petrie said. He passed me a bag of barbeque potato chips. I wasn't one to stand on formality. I took the half empty bag and drew out a handful and crunched along with the Reverend Petrie.

I couldn't eat just one. Between chips I acknowledged, "The creek is my favorite place on Earth. This may not make sense, but at the creek I gained a sense of nature and how I fit in the big picture of creation. I became conscious of my own mortality. It was there that I found an awareness of life and death. Once or twice I had a Saint Francis-like mystic experience at the creek that I never felt in a lifetime of attending church," I stopped and considered what I had just said. "Don't take that the wrong way. I really like your church."

"I know what you mean and for the record it's not my church. It's God's," he made clear. I looked around at the organized mess of his office. I figured he was in the middle of preparing for a sermon. There were books, a Bible and a legal pad reminiscent of Dr. Hayes' on his desk. Crumpled up balls of paper cluttered the floor and overflowed the wastebasket. I liked the notion that a normal person could function amid garbage and disarray.

"Point taken," I said. "Oh, and by the way I read the Saint Francis book and didn't harm it in any way. I have it in the car. I'll go get it in a minute."

"Don't worry about it," Father Petrie said. "If you promise not to cut it up, I'd like for you to keep it."

"I'd like that. Thank you."

"You're welcome. I don't get the sense you were finished talking about the creek," he said.

"That's pretty much all I was going to say. I guess I go on too much about the creek. I just love it there. It's beautiful, peaceful, and spiritual. I escape reality there while at the same time I feel like I'm a little part of God's creation. I've always felt like the creek empowered me."

"Steve, as it turns out, you're quite correct. Freud wrote about a concept he called the Oceanic Feeling. Many people, perhaps the good doctor himself, have had experiences similar to what you just described, except at the ocean. The thrust of the theory is this. Freud believed that people could connect with nature in a way that allowed them to commune with God. In the experience you surrender a part of yourself while at the same time you become one with the greater world around you."

"That's it.  That's what happens to me at the creek.  You couldn't have described it more perfectly," I said with excitement.

"I have a book about that somewhere around here.  Would you like to borrow it?" he asked.

"I would.  More than that, I really want to go back to the creek in a bad way, but I'm afraid," I said.

"Afraid of what?"

"Change."

## Chapter 58

On days like these I cherish Dr. Hayes for making me write in this journal. It really has been a saving grace since I made the dumb ass decision to stop seeing her. My need for a knowledgeable and caring therapist is a topic for another journal entry. Today I have a heavy heart. I need to get it out.

It all started when I arrived at the house on Thanksgiving around midmorning of a beautiful brisk fall day. We had a plan that called for all the guys to pitch in and cook a grand Turkey Day dinner together. However, when I got there I found a woman in the living room. That was a violation of the cardinal rule; no guests, and especially no women. Before I could escort her out, one of the guys handed me a copy of the newspaper. The cover story featured a tale of winter holidays from the perspective of living on the street. There, above the fold of the paper, was a photo of the woman in the living room.

I quickly learned the guys had read the story and went out and found the homeless woman. They brought her back to share in our holiday feast. For all of my human forecasting, I never saw that coming. I felt like Duke's life lesson had not been lost after all. These guys, supposedly the lowest of the low, made a gallant effort to care for their own. In light of the situation and the holiday spirit I relented and allowed the woman to stay. We cooked, prayed, ate and had a wonderful evening together.

Here's the rub. I had missed the first act of kindness and it knocked me for a loop. The next blow knocked my senses back into me. The following day I came to the house to find the

woman there, again. She sat curled up in a corner
of the porch. I knew this was going to be a
problem. It already was one, worse than I realized.
As I approached, prepared to ask her to leave, I
realized she was bruised and bleeding.

"What happened?" I asked.

She shook her head as if to say nothing. I
pushed through the door of the house to find it in
shambles. A couple of the guys looked as bad as
the woman. Out in back, two others were still cock
fighting.

"What the hell is going on here?" I
demanded.

"Aw, you know it, Youngblood. These old
fools found the bitch, they feed her and then they
fucked her. Now they're fighting over her," Doc
said.

Almost all of the fellows encircled the two
fighters yelling and taunting them. I felt a melee on
the horizon. I pulled out my little twenty five
caliber pistol and fired it into the air. The fighting
stopped and all heads whipped into my direction.

"Now that I have your attention; does
somebody want to tell me what in the world is
going on here?"

"Gun. What's this gun stuff? Man, I don't
know you at all. I just lost a lot of respect for you,"
one of the two fighters said, while tending his
bleeding and rapidly swelling eye.

"Respect for me!" I howled. "Get ready,
you're about to lose the rest of it. You need to get
your stuff and get out. Now!" I ordered, still
brandishing the gun.

"Say, lighten up there, Youngblood," Doc
said. "It's like this, you can have a big old pot of

soup that will feed the world and some old fool will fill his bowl and then spit in it."

I didn't feel like thinking about philosophy of life. I turned to the woman. "I need to take you away from here. You can't come back, ever."

We drove for some time without speaking. I pulled up in front of a battered women's shelter. I knew several of the case workers there. I figured she could get cleaned up and some medical attention there. Yet, she refused to go inside.

"I done been there before. They can't help me," she said.

"Fine. Do what you want," I said without argument.

As she exited the car I called to her, "If you want, I can do something about what happened to you."

She didn't respond. So I clarified, "I can call the police if you want," I paused and added. "Or I can take care of it myself."

"Naw, baby. Them mens got it bad enough and it don't look like they gonna get any better no time soon. They'll get theirs. Besides, it's my fault. I shouldn't have come back. I knew no good could come of it," she admitted.

I needed more. I started the car and drove straight to Susannah's house. There, I learned another lesson. I knew better than to try and hide one emotion with another. After I'd shared the difficult tale with her, we made love, and we made a mistake.

Even though I thought the guys committed one of the worst things imaginable. I forged on and kept working with the group. I forced four guys to leave the house and the program over the issue. I saw each of them out on the streets from time to time.  I thought about how the Carpenters had provided a chance for me.  Then I realized these guys had received at least the one chance that I knew of, and probably plenty before that.  They weren't ready for recovery.  I guess some people never are.  Recovery is incredibly hard work, as is supporting that immense task.  I wished it could have been different.  It wasn't.

After a while, we got back into a groove at the house, but it really never was the same.  I didn't trust the group and they knew it.  We lived with a tension that at any given moment could have snapped into an all out war.

## Chapter 59

A small figurine of Buddha sat on Father Petrie's cluttered desk. It was a new acquisition in the constantly changing office. I often wondered if the room ever remained the same for two consecutive days. An inscription at the marble base of the statuette read: *You will not be punished for your anger. You will be punished by your anger.*

"Aren't you afraid the Buddha will offend somebody here at the church?" I asked.

"It was a gift from a parishioner. I felt obligated to put it out here or in the rectory. This seemed like a better place to me," Father Petrie quipped. "Besides, most people in this congregation have open minds, and I can't say I care if it offends the others." We shared a laugh.

"Do you think the quote is true?" I asked.

"Yes," the pastor stopped and thought. "Yes, I think it's absolutely true. Come on, it's too pretty of a day to be inside." Father Petrie got up and walked out. I didn't talk. I just followed him out to the meditation pond behind the church. We sat on the cool stone bench for a minute without continuing the conversation. I saw my reflection in the pond and looked away. I took note of a couple of people passing in the parking lot. I had no idea how many people came by the church on non-worship days. It was like a regular place of business.

"If that quote is true, what am I supposed to do?" I asked.

"You keep going the way you always have."

"I can't live with the knowing that in most ways life was better for me when I buried my pain than it is now when I do all this processing that is supposed to help me," I said.

"From what you've told me, back when you buried your pain you did that by hurting others. You have to know that you can't just go around inflicting pain because you are hurting," Father Petrie said.

"Okay, so in the future I'll be more selective and only hurt those who deserve it."

"Don't be ridiculous," he said.

""I'm not. I feel like pain is my genesis and in twelve verses I'm going to rain down an awful storm."

"Nice symbolism. I know you've had a stay in the wilderness. You've got to find way to see that you're on the other side now."

"There has been a cross over, but I think I ended up on the wrong side."

"I can see how that might happen, but is it what you really want?" Father Petrie asked.

"No. I want atonement," I said. "I want redemption. I want balance. I know words and scripture can't take away what I've done. The truth is that I feel certain I'll do more in the time to come. I know that I'm not a savior. I'm a walking nightmare. Jesus died on the cross to save people from sinners like me. But I also know that there are people worse than me out there."

"I have no doubt that there are people worse than you out there. What worries me is the unbelievable amount of anger and guilt you carry around. Your secret doesn't have to own you any more. Albeit not by your choice, your story is out. Really it's better than the sacrament of confession. Your secret was shared widely. After you told me your story, I remembered hearing about it on

television. But don't worry; you were a minor then
and only a limited number of people remember
stories and faces from one newscast to the next.
When you acted out in school and in the group
home you were directly responding to your life's
situation. Since then you have made good choices.
You've moved forward in life. You have to believe
me. Your past doesn't own you anymore."

"I hear what you are saying and I want to
believe it's all true. Inside I know I have moved on,
but it's not enough. It's like this. My brother used
to punch the cinderblock walls in the basement of
our old house. Duke would tell me it was to
toughen up his hands so he'd be a better fighter. He
would hit it again and again, leaving bloodstains
and skin on the wall. Duke said the more he did it,
the stronger he became. I think Dr. Hayes would
say he was hurting himself and that was the point.
He brought physical pain to his fists to tear his mind
away from the mental and emotional anguish he
endured. Well, I have pain, too. It hurts just the
same. The difference is that I don't want to hurt
myself when I'm aching; I want to unload my fury
on someone else."

"A while back when we talked about dreams
I failed to mention that dreams help you understand
life and they can help you to heal. Knowing the
source of pain is the first step. In dreams or in real
life the notion of war or fighting can tell you a lot.
It may suggest that you are fighting with yourself
and your own sense of the deep seated instinctive
forces of evil."

"I know good and well that I'm my own
worst enemy. I'm not scared of anything as much
as I am of what is inside of me. Are you saying
that's the cause of all my nightmares?" I asked.

"It's a possibility. We talked about this before with the dream about the ghost. I've thought about that since. Perhaps the ghost in your dream is the shadowy and fearful side of yourself. You need to expose it into full view in order face your fear head on and resolve it. Freud said that his overwhelming fear was his mother. Others say that for them it's a fear of death and dying, as we can't be certain if there is a meaningful afterlife or what that might be like."

"Are you seriously suggesting that I might find something in my dreams and nightmares to help me? I think that would offend some Christians more than the Buddha."

"There's no doubt some people of faith think dreams belong to the realm of magic and mystics. I think you are intelligent enough to know that we are talking about your life and how your own mind works for and against you," Father Petrie said.

"Well, I just don't know much about dreams," I said. "What I do know is I rarely ever like the ones I have. Most of the time, some freaky stuff happens in my dreams like I turn into a bird of prey. I have these long powerful talons that rip my insides out and claw away at my flesh. I don't know why I can't just be normal and sleep peacefully."

"No one knows for sure what controls dreams, but we all have them. Trying to make sense from nightmares and dreams has intrigued humans throughout history. Freud was an early theorist in the field to write about them. He linked many of his theories to a child's relationship to his mother. I'm not sure who was worse with a mommy complex, Freud or Saint Augustine. Both

Sigmund Freud and Saint Augustine spent their careers struggling over good and evil. Both felt evil originated and emanated from women, mothers in particular. At least Freud allowed that the mother's influence might be positive or negative."

I thought of all I had read about Freudian thought. I felt like I sat for the portrait of his classic theories. I had magnum cum laude mother issues. I had toilet issues. I had ego and violence issues. "Why do *you* think we have evil in the world?" I asked.

"My faith leads me to believe that God allows evil to bring good from it," Father Petrie said.

"What good came from the Holocaust?" I snapped.

"That's a fair question that you need to explore over many years on your faith journey," the pastor said.

"I think that's the first time you've taken the easy road and punted. It doesn't suit you," I said frankly. "Furthermore, I read Augustine as saying that people are exposed to evil due to their own defects. I think he was saying we suffer evil because we inflict it on ourselves," I said.

"God created humans so we could be fruitful, multiply and prosper, not just to allow us to self destruct," Father Petrie said.

"So says Genesis, but the book of Job chapter two, verse ten asks, "What? Shall we receive good at the hand of God, and shall we not receive evil?"

"You certainly do know your Bible," Father Petrie said.

"There's something to be said for the Baptist Church." I paused, watching a delivery truck pull up into the church's driveway.

"That's the truth. Tell me, who do you connect with the most from the Bible?"

"Are we finished talking about good, evil and dreams and the like?" I asked.

"Don't be a smart aleck. Answer the question."

I didn't need time to think. I launched in to an answer. "The Carpenters and I created interfaith holiday decorations at their house. My contribution was an empty manger. I chose that as I thought about how it must have been for Mary and Joseph. They had to place their precious newborn baby in a musty and dirty old barn. Undoubtedly, the place was cold, filled with animal feces and spiders. I want to believe Jesus began his life in this world just like me."

"Wow, you said a lot in that one. Interesting that you added the spiders. We keep coming back to fear. Your arachnophobia may be a primordial instinctive fear."

"I'm not afraid of spiders. I kill them," I insisted.

"Yes, so you've told me," Father Petrie said as he pulled a handful of weeds growing beside the legs of the bench. "Let's focus on the positive. Are there other ways you see yourself like Jesus?"

"Yes. Like him, I feel capable of doing both great and terrible things."

## Chapter 60

One Saturday afternoon in the late spring the
guys and I were sitting on the porch. The pungent
smell of freshly mowed grass lifted on the afternoon
breeze. We had just finished working on the lawn
and the fellows were telling their horror stories
about the full catastrophe of their lives. Suddenly,
we all perked up at the familiar sound of music. A
jingle with no words filled the mid-morning air.
The nostalgically pleasing sounds came from an ice
cream truck. The thought of cold sweet treats
refreshed us mentally as the music drew near.
Small children emerged from houses and back yards
and ran into the street. We all knew the joy
associated with the melody.

"Ice cream! It's the ice cream man," we
heard the little girl across the road screaming as she
ran with her hand wrapped around a dollar bill. Her
excitement and joy were a sight to behold. Like the
girl and other kids we filed off the porch and darted
across the yard. Then we scattered, slid, dived and
rolled in the loose blades of grass clippings.

Tat tat. Tat tat tat ripped the delight of the
ice cream tune from the air and filled our ears and
minds with confusion and fear. The ice cream truck
came to an abrupt stop. The side door flung open
and gun shots rang out. Blasts of smoke and sparks
leaped out of long black gun barrels as the driver
and another guy in the front seat were firing
automatic weapons. A total of three gunmen shot
repeatedly and wildly into one of the crack houses.
The shooters seemed prepared for Armageddon.
Bullets kept smashing into the house with their
deadly force.

My mind didn't bother with the incongruous bloodshed emanating from a magnet of childhood bliss. I focused my eyes on my car. I had a gun under the seat. The six shot pistol was no match for this three man army. No matter, I felt sure I could make it to the car, as the shooters were purposefully firing at the house across the street. I did make it. Once there, I stopped. It wasn't because I came to my senses and decided to avoid imminent suicide. It wasn't because the firing mercifully stopped. I stopped to pray. I prayed for the little girl still clutching her ice cream money who lay writhing in pain. I could hear her screaming in agony through the ear piercing gun fire. The spray of bullets mercifully came to an end. I ran toward the girl. The gunmen ignored me. A woman came running from the house. She wailed and waved her arms as she ran. She dove on top of the girl. The child's crying stopped seconds before her mother arrived. Her blood stained dollar bill tumbled into the street amid the spent shells. I prayed some more.

## Chapter 61

For seventeen days I stayed in a monastery.
I read a book on meditation that said unspoken
desires and fantasies can be linked to issues of
power or a lack thereof. The words reverberated in
my mind as I had been mentally acting out how to
right the latest atrocity I had witnessed. I felt more
impulsively violent than ever before, but my actions
were really being driven by my deep compulsions.
The brothers tried to console me, but those were
tricky times. I knew if I denied the feelings roving
through my body, then they'd escape for the
moment and pop up somewhere else. If I expressed
them, I feared getting in over my head. I decided to
take it slowly. The excess time I offered myself as
a gift to overcome impulse slowly turned into a
curse. I began to methodically plan out my violent
reaction.

I went to the city and closed the house. In
my absence vandals had ripped out all the copper
tubing in the walls and crawl space, everything,
even the toilets had been removed or smashed.
Graffiti decorated the walls with profane words and
pictures. Threats to my life were drafted on the
floors and on the ceilings. I took what I could
salvage and walked away. My plan was to return it
to the center and quit my job.

Across the street I saw the slain little girl's
mother sitting on porch. I paused. Then I opened
my car door. I looked over the top of the car and
my eyes caught the curbside memorial marker with
a pink heart and flowers, fresh flowers. I closed the
door and walked across the street. My whole life
had been about choices. Many of them were
beyond my means of control. The outcome and

consequences of those choices shaped me regardless of how they were set in motion. For all the good, bad and indifference I had known, today all I could think about was taking care of my own. More than once I had tried to do the noble thing, but some time you have to let nature run its course.

"I saw what happened here. I saw what happened to your daughter," I said. The woman acknowledged my words with a gentle nod of her head. She said nothing. I continued, "I can't take away your pain, but if you want I can introduce the families of those men to the same grief that has been visited on you."

The woman twisted in her chair. She looked to be in her very early twenties. "I thought you were some kind of preacher. You helping those men and all."

"No ma'am. Whatever I was before…well I'm not anymore," I said, not looking directly at her. Stillness ruled the moment.

"Something's not right here. You tryin' to play me or something?" she said.

"No, ma'am. I shouldn't have said anything. Just forget about it. I'm sorry about your loss. The flowers are definitely beautiful. It's a nice tribute to her." I turned and walked away, thinking about what I had just done. What was I thinking? What did I expect her to say? I felt sick.

"Hey!" the voice of the dead girl's mother shot though the moment, through me.

I turned and looked straight into her pain soaked eyes. I felt the tenderness of the love she had for her daughter. I tasted the bitterness of the loss she couldn't explain. I understood and I sensed her reading me as she held my gaze and nodded. I

pressed my lips, walked to car and never looked
back.

## Chapter 62

Somehow I feel certain this will be my last journal entry for some time, if not the last one ever. I sat in the courtyard of the monastery and listened to water trickle down an impressive fountain. I tried to focus my energies on reading a book of Freudian interpretations of dreams. I found the book in the reading room. I thought it seemed like strange reading material for such a place. Equally as strange was my reading of the book, as I had hardly slept at all. I noticed the slightest little movement out of the corner of my eye. It was as I thought, as I dreaded. A spider ambled along the bench next to me.

I slid over next to the spider and began talking very calmly to it. I didn't dare make a scene in front of the brothers. I gave the spider my same old spiel, minus the rage. Then without thinking, I placed my hand, palm up, in the spider's path. I invited the beast to join me. I had seen others do this and it had always given me the creeps. Many people made mention of how spiders rarely ever attack. They say if you take a spider into your hand you can humanely relocate it to the more appropriate place outside. I was told this nearly every time after I had annihilated a spider. Today seemed like a good day to put that theory to the test.

The spider slowly climbed on my finger. For a creature that bordered on weightless, it rendered my arm immobile. I felt each of its tiny legs moving as if porcupine quills jabbed into my hand marking the spider's path. I couldn't breathe. I stopped my idle chatter with the thing. Hot and cold sensations ran over my body. I felt ready to collapse under the weight of the insignificant little

spider that had now moved midway along my
finger. Inhale. Exhale. I needed to own this
moment.

"You don't know me," I explained to the
spider. "You may not have a god. The Good Book
of my faith says the son will toil for the father's sin.
You should know that you have an ancestor. Many
years ago the two of us had a stormy encounter in
the middle of the night. Your ancestor escaped.
The encounter you and I are having is close to the
end. You will not escape."

The very book I had been reading suggested
that spiders symbolize fear. It said that those who
detest spiders may feel ensnared in a web of lies or
entangled by something horrifying that cannot be
escaped. Another suggestion was that the one who
fears spiders may well be the one casting the web to
trap and torment others. Finally, in his classic style,
Freud said that spiders in dreams represented
mothers who devour their children with
possessiveness or guilt. I knew all too well that
mothers are capable of cruelty. I wondered what on
Earth Mrs. Freud had done to her son.

For half of my life I had been killing spiders.
I made every effort not to touch them. I knocked
them down with something and then stomped them
under the soles of my shoes. Today, in contrast, I
went toe to toe with my fear. For a change, I altered
the game and gave the spider an option. It could
choose to bite me. In any event, death loomed
imminently. Today the big difference would be that
the spider's end would come in my bare hand, not
the sole of my shoe or with some impromptu
swatter. Today, it was just me and the spider. And
so it ended.

## Chapter 63

Once I left the monastery I knew what needed to be done and I had no intention of wasting anymore time. I called my old friend JT Cook, the private investigator. He, like everybody else under the sun, had heard about the ice cream truck incident. He was appalled. After I recounted my eyewitness version he happily agreed to help me.

"I need a gun that can't be traced," I told him.

"That's not my realm of expertise," he said. "I have a reputation and more importantly, a state licensure to keep. I think you can find what you need via other avenues. The kid I knew was very resourceful. I don't think you've changed that much. Maybe you are even more resourceful now than you were back then."

"I hear you. I know a guy." I thought of how scripted that sounded. It didn't matter. I did know a guy. It would take a dollar or two, but I knew for certain that Bubba would be able to take care of me.

"The police have determined the shooters were not from the rival house," JT said.

"Hell, all they had to do was ask. We had never seen them before," I said.

"My guess is the guys are from the distribution source. I think they probably got tired of the traffic in the area getting stepped on so they took it out."

"I can buy into that," I agreed.

"The truck. That will be their undoing. I'll get on it," JT said confidently.

He proved why he had such a stellar reputation as an investigator. JT did just as he said.

In under thirty-six hours gave me a lead on the guys
from the truck. I took my turn next. I mingled the
good with the bad. Like the spider that is a hero for
eliminating insects to some, it had always been a
terrorist to me. Within the next twenty-four hours I
took up the same two pronged fork and eliminated
that which I recognized as a problem.

## Chapter 64

"When I got you that last one you gave me all kind of lip about guns being for sissies. How is it all of a sudden you need a piece without a history? What's up?" Bubba asked.

"I've got a thing to take care of."

"A thing, huh? Must be a big thing," he said.

"It's no big deal. It's the same reason as the other gun, there may come a time when I need to get and hold a couple two three people's attention."

"You can get attention with the gun you have," Bubba said and handed me a beer. "I don't imagine you care if I believe you or not?"

"Not really," I said. "For the record, I won't use the gun, not on a person. This thing I need to handle…it has to be face to face. Not at a distance. We've got to be accountable, get my hands dirty."

"Sounds personal," Bubba said. "Mostly, it sounds dramatic. Are you looking for an Oscar for that line?"

"Nope. Looking for retribution."

"Ooo. Use that one instead for Oscar consideration," Bubba joked.

"Man, I'm not in a humorous mood. Can you hook me up or not?"

"I've got you covered. You need help with this thing of yours?"

"No. I'm good for now. I'll let you know as the time gets closer."

"Sounds to me like you know that time's coming pretty soon," Bubba said.

I looked at my watch. "It'll be over shortly. Are we going to play pool or not?" I asked.

"It's your dime, Fat Boy.  You want to pony up the ten spot now or wait 'till you lose?"

## Chapter 65

I couldn't calm down. I was worked up unlike anything I'd ever known before. I was volatile, too volatile. Nurture and nature predisposed me to hostility and pain. They circulated in my genes and upbringing. They shaped me into what I had become. I had used it. Now I had the responsibility of channeling it. I thought about how I have to use it. What else am I fit to do? I've always heard it's not where you come from, but what you do. I figured I'd feel differently once it was done. I held no guilt, no pain, no sorrow. I just felt the satisfaction of completing a task. I did it and it was done.

I used to internalize everything. That gave me stomachaches. I worked it out in the form of aggression and violence. Now I know the poison I'm dealing with and have taken precautions when handling it. I told myself venom can be an antidote to some and deadly to others. That's me, I can be both. I don't want to die, but I'm tired of living with the agony of my existence. I'm going to bring terror to those who terrorize.

I have repeatedly claimed that I know pain. I know how it feels. I can endure pain. I know how to inflict pain. I know that each of us can find ourselves hurting and it is only bringing pain to others that can ease that deep aching. I decided to use that for both the blessed and condemned.

Tension between sin and righteousness, right and wrong and nature verses nurture ruled me for years. I had all the makings of a serial killer. I wanted to do better, to be better. I wanted to transcend the ugliness of my rearing, of my bloodline. I had no idea how that was supposed to happen. Everything inside of me weighed in on the other side. The fight took its toll on me and I grew weary of wondering if it was so wrong to be what I was born into. I've grown exhausted of the hostile environment that surrounds me. I have crossed over to the dark side. Now each and every day I have to act and react accordingly to keep from becoming lost.

My whole life converged in one moment, in one action. It left me manic. In my mania I had nowhere else to go. I drove to the creek. I passed the sign bearing the creek's name. I remembered the long night when I got picked up in MD's basement. My return trip to the creek found the beach area completely submerged. God, does nothing avoid the swinging hand of change? The creek was consistently exposed to change, yet its waters continued to flow every day.

In one of our talks about dreams Father Petrie pointed out that nearly every creation story across cultures began with water. Oceans, rivers, and creeks, along with chaos, existed before man. All of them, especially chaos, continue despite man. Father Petrie said his old professor taught that mystically water represented feelings and emotions. The unconscious, like changes in our lives, flows every minute of every day. They are the forces of life. The pastor said the moral of the story was to go with the flow rather than struggling. In the dream book at the monastery I read that crossing over water has symbolic meaning for fundamental change. Crossing Carp Bridge the very first time I came to the creek, that cold winter day in the back seat of the Granada on my way to foster care and today all brought a world of change.

Since that first time when Duke left me to swim or drown I yearned to be one with the creek. It was the one beautiful thing I knew. When God saw fit to unleash fury on the natural world, I felt the creek's pain as its waters became swollen, drained or cluttered. When God punished me, I sat on the creek's bank and swallowed my own pain. I tried to learn about the creek and the life it sustained. I longed to be as noble.

I waded into the water fully clothed and fell to my knees. I joined the creek as my tears trickled into the water. I looked up and prayed for the sky to part and a dove of peace to descend on my baptism of tears and living water. Blood, tears and fire. My baptism wasn't a stand alone event. I experienced the sacrament by way of water, blood and fire. I remember Pastor Frank saying, "You must endure death and destruction to gain rebirth." The water the preacher dunked me in was warmer and I felt a sight more pious then than I did standing waist deep in the cool running creek.

I wrung my blood soaked hands and looked down and saw my own reflection in the water. It moved, yet I stood still. The guy in the watery mirror seemed like a stranger. Oddly enough, I knew him. I understood the distorted fellow to be me. Seeing myself gave me an initial response much different from that of Narcissus on his first glimpse of his own image. I found no vanity. I certainly didn't see any likeness of nobility, but I felt a slight twinge of liberation.

And so I began.

www.ingramcontent.com/pod-product-compliance
Lightning Source LLC
Chambersburg PA
CBHW050501260626
47157CB00004B/1136